S0-AER-405

BLIND DATE

BLIND DATE

James Pattinson

NEW HANOVER COUNTY
PUBLIC LIBRARY
201 CHESTNUT STREET
WILMINGTON, NC 28401

CHIVERS
THORNDIKE

This Large Print edition is published by BBC Audiobooks Ltd, Bath, England and by Thorndike Press®, Waterville, Maine, USA.

Published in 2004 in the U.K. by arrangement with Robert Hale Limited.

Published in 2004 in the U.S. by arrangement with Robert Hale Limited.

U.K. Hardcover ISBN 0–7540–7795–0 (Chivers Large Print)
U.K. Softcover ISBN 0–7540–7796–9 (Camden Large Print)
U.S. Softcover ISBN 0–7862–6337–7 (Nightingale)

Copyright © James Pattinson 1978

All rights reserved.

The text of this Large Print edition is unabridged.
Other aspects of the book may vary from the original edition.

Set in 16 pt. New Times Roman.

Printed in Great Britain on acid-free paper.

British Library Cataloguing in Publication Data available

Library of Congress Control Number: 2003116421

CONTENTS

CONTENTS

CHAPTER ONE

OFF THE HOOK

They were waiting for him in an alleyway which went by the name of Lord's Walk and was about as unlordly as could well have been imagined. There were dirty brick walls on each side with a lot of graffiti chalked on them, or imprinted rather more indelibly with aerosol paint, the compulsive wall-defiler's newest weapon. Brady had read some of the inscriptions in daylight and might well have been shocked if he had not long since lost the capacity to absorb shock from any kind of written message or crude illustration.

Mixed in with the coarser material were such slogans as 'Bring back the rope' and 'Pensions for school-leavers', and there was also the bold statement: 'Adolf Hitler is alive and well and teaching maths at Lee Road Comprehensive'. Which looked like the basis for a few searching inquiries on the part of the Greater London education authorities.

As soon as Brady saw the two men he had the feeling that he was in for trouble, and he felt half inclined to make a smart about turn and move swiftly away in the opposite direction. But then he thought: Why in hell should I? And he went on. Maybe they were not waiting for him anyway; maybe they were just standing there and having a quiet talk about this and that before going off home to bed. But he knew he was just kidding himself.

They let him get right up to them before they made a move. He made as if to pass them, but the bigger of the two shifted a couple of steps to the left and stood dead in his way. Brady came to a halt and looked at the men, not able to see them too clearly in the light that was provided in Lord's Walk, but clearly enough. The one who had moved to block his path had slightly hunched shoulders and a head like a large round pudding seated on them. The other man was less heavily built; he looked bony; he had a long face, long arms and big bony hands. He was not doing anything with the hands; not yet. There was no one else in sight.

It was the big man who spoke. 'In a hurry, Mr Brady?' He had a snuffling kind of voice and he breathed noisily, as if there were some obstruction in his nose.

'Yes,' Brady said.

'You can spare a few minutes, though?'

'What do you want?'

'A word, Mr Brady, just a word.'

'Is that all?'

'Well, it depends, don't it?'

'On what?'

'On whether you're going to act sensible. We don't want trouble no more than you do.

So 'ow about it?'

'I think you'll have to explain that,' Brady said. 'What exactly would acting sensible involve? I'm a bit in the dark.'

'Don't give us that,' the bony man put in. He had a snappish way of speaking, as though his temper might flare up on the slightest provocation. 'You know what we're here for, so don't play the little innocent.'

Brady wondered whether it would be possible to keep things going in the verbal line until someone came along, but he doubted it. And even if someone did come along the charces were that he would get very little help; most people had a way of thinking twice, or even three or four times, before getting mixed up in other citizens' affairs, especially when two of those other citizens were such obvious hard cases as these. What he really needed was a policeman, but policemen seemed to be rather thin on the ground in that particular area at that hour of the night. They were probably all riding round in Pandas or Z-cars and not caring a damn what happened to one, Stephen Brady, in Lord's Walk—or anywhere else if it came to the point.

'You'd better tell me just the same,' he said.

'All right,' the big man said. He seemed to be a shade more reasonable than the bony one, a little less on a hair-trigger. 'All right, I'll tell you. Acting sensible would be giving us four 'underd an' fifty quid, that's what acting sensible would be. Just you 'and over the money, Mr Brady, and then we all go 'ome 'appy.'

'And if not?'

'If not we 've to get nasty. No 'ard feelings, mind. It's just a job, see?'

'Well,' Brady said, 'it's nice to know there aren't any hard feelings involved. That makes me a whole lot happier.'

'You won't be happier if you don't cough up,' the bony man said. 'You'll be bleedin' unhappy.'

Brady looked past the big man and he could see where Lord's Walk came to an end not more than twenty yards away. If he could slip past and make it as far as that he might stand a chance of getting clean away, but he knew they were watching him closely and the moment he made the smallest move they would be on to him like a couple of angry gorillas.

'You're acting on behalf of a third party, of course,' he said. 'You're not wanting the money just for yourselves?'

'You know the score,' the bony man said. 'So why don't we cut the cackle? Are you going to pay up or do we have to get to work on you?'

'Why don't we go to my place? You don't expect me to carry sums like that around with me, do you?'

The bony man spoke to his companion. 'He's just stalling. Let's get it over with. Let's

4

quit fooling around. It's getting late.'

The big man gave a nod with his pudding head and his breathing sounded louder. His right arm shot out suddenly like a piston getting to work and the clenched fist hit Brady in the pit of the stomach. He ought to have avoided it; he had been anticipating something of the kind; and yet the speed of the big man had taken him by surprise. If a small bomb had exploded in front of him he doubted whether it could have had a more devastating effect; it was as though his intestines had been rolled into a ball and slammed up against his backbone; and he was not at all sure they might not have been driven clean out the other side. He had no time to give it much thought, however, because something hit him on the side of the jaw and he was already falling before he had come to the conclusion that it must have been the big man's other fist.

He had never realised quite how hard the surface of Lord's Walk was until then; he had never felt any inclination to test it with his shoulder and would not have done so then if he had been offered any choice in the matter. It was, he discovered, an extremely unresilient surface; it did no good at all to his left shoulder, or any other part of that side of his body, either. And then, as if things had not been bad enough already, the bony man had to join in with a viciously aimed boot in the ribs. Or it could have been a shoe. Either way it was nasty, very nasty indeed. And the trouble was, it was likely to get worse the longer it went on.

He tried to get up, but the big man planted a foot on his chest and held him down while the bony one put the boot in again, or the shoe, or whatever it was, and it looked like turning into a long, hard session of much unpleasantness. And maybe it would have done just that if there had not been an interruption.

Someone said: 'Stop that!'

There was a certain peremptoriness in the way in which those two brief words were uttered which left no doubt in the mind that they were meant to be obeyed, and promptly. The two men stopped it.

Brady had not heard anyone approaching. He had been completely unaware of the arrival of this fourth party until the order had been rapped out, and he could scarcely believe it even then. It was difficult to be absolutely certain on the evidence of just two words, but he had a feeling that he recognised the voice, though it seemed so improbable as to be practically inconceivable. For what on earth would she be doing in that unlikely place at that unlikely time of night?

And then she said, still in that very peremptory tone of voice: 'Get away from him, both of you. Stand over there against the wall. Move it.'

They moved it, and Brady knew that he had

6

been right the first time: it was indeed Linda Manning; and when the men had shifted clear of his line of vision he could see that she was holding a gun in her right hand. He would have made a bet, too, that it was the one she sometimes carried around in her handbag, along with the driving licence and the keyring and the cosmetics and the loose change; the small automatic which he had seen on quite a few previous occasions and which he knew she could use very effectively when the need arose. His surprise at seeing her did not make him any the less pleased about it, because she had certainly stepped in at the right moment and saved him from a pretty painful going-over, whatever the reason for her being there might have been.

She glanced down at him. 'Don't you think it might be as well to get up? Or are you planning to spend the night lying there?'

The pain in his stomach was beginning to subside a little and he found that he was able to do as she had suggested. He got to his feet and stood there, feeling a bit sore and groggy but better than he might have been, a great deal better. The gun was still pointing at the two men and they were still standing by the wall and staring at it as though it fascinated them.

'Lady,' the big man said, and he sounded nervous, 'why don't you put that gun away? Nobody ain't going to do you no 'arm, straight.'

'Nobody's going to have the chance,' she said. She made no move to put the automatic away; she spoke to Brady again, but without taking her attention for a moment off the other two. 'Is there anything you'd like to say to these gentlemen before we let them go? Any little score you'd like to settle?'

Brady was fairly sure she was not referring to money matters, and he had half a mind to walk across and give his assailants a few choice kicks on the shins by way of an exchange for what he himself had undergone. But he was not really feeling quite up to it, and where was the point in making enemies anyway?

He shook his head. 'I've said all I want to say to them.'

'Well, if you're sure about that,' she said, and she made a gesture of dismissal with the gun. 'Beat it.'

The two men beat it.

Miss Manning put the automatic back in her handbag.

'Nice seeing you again,' Brady said. And he meant it; not only because she had got him out of a very sticky situation but also because it was always nice to see her, even if the sight of her did give him the uneasy feeling that he was about to be coerced into doing something his better judgement told him he ought not to touch with the longest barge-pole that had ever been made.

She did not reply by echoing his sentiments.

She just said: 'Let's skip the greetings, shall we? I think we'd better go back to that squalid dump you call a flat. It hasn't become any less nauseating, I see.'

'You mean you've been there?'

'It's where I've been for the last three hours—waiting. I finally ran out of patience—luckily for you, as it happened.'

'I'd like to thank you for that.'

'All right, so you've thanked me.'

'How did you get into the flat? With a skeleton key?'

'There was no need for anything quite so melodramatic. Your landlady opened the door for me and said it would be all right if I waited there until you came back.'

'Oh, she did, did she?'

'Don't let it worry you. She said she wouldn't do it for just anyone, but she knew Mr B would want her to make an exception in my case.'

'I wonder what gave her that idea.'

'I think she likes me. She also seems to think it's time you got yourself hooked up with a nice sensible young lady, because that might be the making of you.'

'She reads too many romantic novels,' Brady said. 'They give her the strangest ideas. It's a good thing she doesn't know what you do for a living.'

'Possibly so. Anyway, I think we ought to be moving. That's if you feel capable of walking.'

9

He detected more than a hint of mockery and it stung him to remark: 'I don't think you give a damn whether I've suffered some permanent injury or not.'

'Oh, but you're wrong,' she said. 'I do care. After all, what good would you be to me as a cripple, Steve? What good at all?'

He was not sure he liked the sound of that; it had a faintly sinister overtone. It seemed to indicate that he was only too right in thinking that she had turned up again with another of those propositions which sent cold shivers rippling along his spine. Maybe it might not be a bad idea to feign a limp or something by way of insurance—life insurance. Only he doubted whether he would get away with it; she was not easily fooled.

'Come along then,' she said.

He scrapped the idea of a limp and went along.

*   *   *

They walked into the house and climbed the stairs to the flat, and when he switched the light on he took a good look at the place, trying to see it as someone else might. After he had done so he had to admit to himself that Linda Manning had not been far out in describing it as nauseating: it was not exactly in the luxury class at the best of times, but lately it seemed to have taken on a little extra dinginess. He remembered when she had brought a man named Stewart Cobb to see him. Cobb had been a fastidious person and had seemed reluctant even to sit down for fear of contamination. Well, he would never come there again; he had turned out to be a treacherous bastard for all his smooth talk and his expensive tailoring, and he had paid for his treachery with his life. Which was a lesson of some kind, Brady supposed.

'Would you care for any refreshment?' he asked. 'There's some canned beer, or I could make a cup of coffee—instant variety.'

She gave him a quick inspection and he noted that her eyes were just as dark and lustrous as they had been the last time he had seen her; which was not altogether surprising, since there was no good reason why they should have changed to any great extent in the course of six months or so. She was not wearing a hat and the jet-black hair was done in one of those styles which were intended to give the impression that nothing whatever had been done. She probably forked out quite a bit to get that effect, and the chocolate-brown trouser suit was not the kind you picked up for thirty or forty pounds, either. So they were obviously still paying her very nicely for the work she did and she appeared to be thriving on it.

'Don't you think,' she said, 'that I'd better make the coffee while you get yourself cleaned up a bit? If you'll forgive my saying so, you're not looking quite up to the mark.'

'Frankly, I'm not feeling quite up to the mark, either.'

'Right then. I suppose you still keep things in the same place?' She put her handbag down on the table and moved towards the kitchenette.

'Same place,' Brady said. 'And incidentally, I see you still carry that gun around with you.'

She came to a halt and glanced at him over her shoulder. 'There are times when a small firearm can be very useful.'

'I'm not arguing.'

'You shouldn't be. If I'd had no pistol you could have got yourself hurt.'

'I did get myself hurt.'

'I mean badly.'

'It was bad enough for me,' Brady said. But he knew what she meant.

She disappeared into the kitchenette and he could hear her making noises of disgust. Not without reason: he remembered that the sink was full of dirty crockery and that the garbage bucket was so full the lid refused to close. He left her to it and went to the bathroom and had a look at himself in the glass. His jaw was a bit swollen and discoloured where the big man's fist had struck it, but it could have been worse. There was some dirt from Lord's Walk on his jacket and trousers, but most of it could probably be sponged off. Not so bad really.

But what about next time? They would hardly leave it at that; they would catch him again, and when they did there might be no Linda Manning to step in and save him from punishment. Well, there was nothing he could do about it; he could hardly hand over four hundred and fifty pounds which he did not possess. He gave a sigh and slipped out of the jacket.

By the time he had finished cleaning himself up she had the coffee ready.

'Do you have to live like a pig?' she asked.

'I'm not sure pigs live this way nowadays,' Brady said. 'I think they've gone up in the world.'

'Then why don't you?'

'I don't know.'

'Steve Brady,' she said, 'you're just letting yourself run to seed. Do you know that?'

He thought about it. Maybe she was right; maybe he had been letting things slide.

She sat down in one of the worn-out armchairs with the greasy uncut moquette upholstery and the broken springs. 'You ought to take a grip on yourself, Steve.' She sipped her coffee and looked at him severely. 'Who were those men?'

Brady lowered himself carefully into the other armchair and also drank some coffee. She had remembered how he liked it—just the right amount of coffee, the right amount of milk and the right amount of sugar. In many respects she was a marvellous girl; in almost every respect, in fact. If only she didn't have that way of bringing trouble into his life.

'The big one was Joe Hodges; he used to be known as The Bear when he was on the all-in wrestling circuit. The other one was a useful welter-weight in his day—Mouse-ear Harry Watkins.'

'What have they got against you?'

'Nothing, really.'

'So they were just giving you a hard time for the hell of it?'

'Oh, no; they don't do things like that. It was strictly a business deal; they were carrying out instructions.'

'Whose instructions?'

'A man named Milligan.'

'Why should he want to have you beaten up?'

'He thinks I owe him some money.'

'And do you?'

'Well, I suppose you could say that. He runs a gambling joint. I lost a bit on the tables and gave him a cheque that bounced.'

She gave a slow shake of the head and made tut-tutting noises with her tongue. 'You really do make things hard for yourself, don't you, Steve? What was the amount of the cheque?'

'Four hundred and fifty pounds.'

'You must be crazy. What did you think you were doing?'

'I was trying to raise some capital.'

14

'You chose a fine way of doing that.'

'It might have worked. I was just unlucky.'

'From where I'm sitting it looks more like being plain stupid. Do you often try that method of raising the wind?'

'No. It was just an impulse.'

'And now you're on the hook?'

'Yes.'

'Well,' she said, and she took another mouthful of the coffee as though she really liked it even if it had been brewed in a pigsty, 'it seems, Steve Brady, that this is your lucky night.'

He stared at her suspiciously, knowing there had to be a catch. 'Oh! How do you make that out?'

'We can get you off the hook.'

'Now wait a minute,' Brady said. 'Are you telling me your lot would be willing to pay my gambling debt?'

'I think I can promise that much. Yes, I really think it wouldn't be too much to promise.'

His suspicions deepened. 'And what am I expected to do in return?'

'A little job. A very simple little job. Nothing to it, nothing at all.'

The coffee seemed to have gone sour on him. Or something had.

'I knew it,' he said. 'I just knew there had to be a catch.'

She gave him a sweet smile, got up from the

armchair and set her empty cup down on the table. 'I must go now.'

'Do you have to?'

'Now what are you suggesting?' she asked, one eyebrow lifting.

'I thought you might feel like sticking around and giving me a bit of feminine comfort. Just to ease me over the shock.'

'You don't need comforting. What you need is a good night's sleep. And with me here I'm afraid you might find that difficult to get.'

He could see she had a point there, but for his part he would have been willing to dispense with the sleep; it was a long time since he had made love to her. Too long. There were a lot of pleasant memories mixed in with the other kind.

'Don't you think it's a bit dangerous for a girl like you to be out alone at this time of night?'

'For a girl like me,' she said, 'I don't think it's dangerous at all.'

He thought about the gun in the handbag and had to admit that she was probably right again. She was pretty good at taking care of herself.

'Besides,' she added, with another of those sweet smiles, 'I don't happen to owe anyone four hundred and fifty pounds.'

Brady winced. She was rubbing salt into the wound. 'And you think I'm going to take this job—whatever it is?'

'Oh, you'll take it, Steve; you'll take it. What choice have you got?'

He knew what she was hinting at—that, quite apart from the little matter of what he owed Milligan, they could use pressure if they had to. They had used it before and they would do so again, if necessary; when they called he had to come running. Linda had spoken about getting him off the hook but he was still on this other hook—and always would be until they chose to let him go. Just because he had done a job or two for them—not very well and not very willingly—they seemed to think they had the right to keep him in reserve, on call as it were. Well, thank God they didn't call very often; thank God for that.

'I'll pick you up in the morning,' she said. 'About ten. Be ready.'

Ready for what? he thought. Ready for what? But he didn't ask.

CHAPTER TWO

SHOTGUN WEDDING

She came for him in her car promptly at ten. She had changed it again and this time it was a Lotus Eclat instead of the Spitfire, so it looked as though she was still on the way up.

Mrs Groucher was in the hall doing a bit of work with a bucket of soapy water and a mop. She gave them a big motherly smile. ' 'Aving a day hout? That's nice. Enjoy yourselves when you're young, I always say. You're a long time dead.'

Brady reflected that she might have come up with a remark that struck a slightly less ominous note, but she was full of happy little sayings like that. At least the weather was being kinder than might have been expected in March; the sun was shining and it would have been very pleasant driving around with Linda Manning if the object of the exercise had been somewhat different.

'Who are we going to see this time?' he asked.

She was busy getting the Lotus under way and answered without turning her head: 'Same man. Graham Turner.'

'I thought I was out of favour with him.'

'Because of the mess you made of that

18

last job?'

'I didn't make a mess of it. At any rate, I shouldn't have done if I'd been given a bit more information.'

'Possibly not. But the fact is, Steve, we can't trust people like you with too much information. Sorry to be so blunt, but that's how it is.'

'What do you mean by people like me?'

'Well, you're not a real professional, are you?'

'I never want to be.'

'There you are. That's your attitude. You know you could have had a permanent job with us.'

'Yes, I know.'

'So—'

'It's not my particular cup of tea. Glass of poison might be a more accurate term. The occasional assignment is bad enough, heaven knows, but doing that kind of thing all the time would drive me crackers.'

'I haven't been driven crackers.'

'Maybe that's because it runs in your family. Or so you told me.'

'I told you that? When?'

'A long time ago. Sitting in a black Jaguar on the bank of a canal in Amsterdam.'

She gave him a quick glance. 'You've got a good memory.'

'For things like that—things I've done with you. I remember Finland too. I remember that

19

log cabin of Jaakko Karsten's beside the lake. I remember a honeymoon caper. It was nice, Linda, while it lasted; really nice.'

He thought the colour mounted a little in her cheek, so perhaps she had not entirely forgotten, either. Perhaps she was also remembering how nice it had been.

'It was a long time ago,' she said; with a touch of regret, it seemed.

'Not so very long at that.'

'It seems so.'

'Do you mean it couldn't happen again?'

'I don't think we should talk about it. There are other matters—'

'Like this job I'm to be pushed into?'

'That is the immediate concern, isn't it?'

'And suppose I were to say I can't afford to take the time off from my legimate work?'

She gave a laugh at that. 'Are you telling me you have legitimate work? Have you gone back to the antique trade?'

'I do a bit now and then—on commission.'

'But no regular job?'

He had to admit that there was no regular job. He was pretty sure she had been aware of that already.

'So in fact this couldn't have turned up at a better time for you. We pay your gambling debt and you're in the black again.'

'Has Turner agreed to that?'

'He's agreed.'

'And do I get anything besides? Something

20

to set the ball rolling again.'

'That, I think, will depend on how well you do. There mustn't be any blunders this time, you understand?'

'I don't understand a thing,' Brady said. 'I don't even know what kind of job I have to do.'

'Be patient, Steve. Turner will tell you.'

'I bet he will. And I bet it'll stink.'

'I don't know why you always have to be so gloomy,' she said. 'Anybody would think you were going to a funeral.'

Brady gave a hollow laugh. 'Maybe I am. Mine.'

*   *   *

Turner's office looked exactly the same as it had when Brady had last seen it. Which meant that it was about as tidy as a corporation rubbish dump. Turner matched it; with his flabby, sagging body and his unpressed tweed suit, scuffed shoes and frayed collar, he might have been a candidate for the rubbish dump himself. He had his burnt-down briar pipe going like an incinerator and the room was so full of smoke the air was scarcely breathable.

He greeted Brady as affably as if that unfortunate business in Hungary which had resulted in the death of Mrs Winthrop and the utter failure of a plan to plant a British agent in Moscow had never occurred. His handclasp was warm and there was no indication

21

whatever that he still blamed Brady for the fiasco, as he had certainly done at the time.

'Well now,' he said, lifting a pile of manila folders off one of the chairs and pushing it forward, 'we haven't seen a lot of you lately, have we? Where've you been hiding yourself?'

Brady sat down. 'I haven't been hiding myself anywhere. It's just that you haven't been looking very hard.'

Turner chuckled good-humouredly. 'Possibly not, possibly not. Nothing in your particular line seems to have cropped up—until now.'

'I didn't know I had a particular line,' Brady said.

'You have certain talents.'

'Well, that's nice to know. Are you going to tell me what they are?'

'Now you're being modest. I'm sure you don't need me to tell you that.'

Linda Manning, after a slight struggle, had managed to open the window, and the air became marginally fresher. She moved to the third chair and sat down.

'Don't you think,' she suggested, 'that we might finish with the compliments and get to the point?'

Turner smiled at her benevolently. 'Always eager to get things moving, eh? The impatience of youth.' He sighed, as though regretting that he himself would never again be as youthful and impatient as that.

'I'm not so old, either,' Brady said. 'And I'd

also be glad to hear what you have in mind. You mentioned that something had cropped up.'

'Ah, yes.' Turner shuffled some of the papers on his desk, apparently looking for something. He did not find it, gave up the search and sucked noisily at his pipe. 'Have you ever been to Poland, Mr Brady?'

Brady felt his heart give a lurch. So it was to be that part of the world again—Iron Curtain country. As if he had not had enough of that lark. True, Poland was not the worst of the bunch, but it was Iron Curtain nevertheless, and he wanted none of it.

'No,' he said, 'I've never been there. I've never felt the desire. To tell you the truth, I haven't any desire to go there now.'

'It's a nice country—as Communist countries go.'

'They can't go far enough for my liking. I've heard it's very flat.'

'There are some beautiful cities.'

'Have you seen them?'

'Well, no,' Turner admitted, 'but I've seen pictures. Very good pictures.'

'Suppose I just settle for the pictures, too.'

'That would hardly answer the purpose.'

'I was afraid it wouldn't,' Brady said. 'All right, let's have it. Tell me the worst. In what way do I have to risk my life this time?'

'Oh, there's no risk.' Turner seemed quite taken aback by the mere suggestion that there might be. 'None at all.'

Brady was not convinced. 'That's what you said last time, remember? It was to be a no risk operation, strictly that. And what happened?'

A slight frown crossed Turner's face. It had perhaps been a mistake to remind him of that affair; it might turn him sour again. Though, sweet or sour, what difference did it make?

'That,' Turner said, 'was because you didn't stick to your brief. Nobody told you to go barging across the border into Hungary.'

'I didn't go barging across; I was taken.'

'Only because you had to be so officious.'

'Officious! Well, for crying out loud! I was only doing what you told me to do—keeping an eye on Mrs Winthrop.'

'You weren't told to get quite so involved.'

'Well, if you'd given me a bit more to go on maybe I wouldn't have. You misled me from the start; you said she was one of theirs, not one of yours.'

'That was how it had to be done. If you'd known the facts we couldn't have been sure you'd play your part the right way. Not that you did, as it turned out.'

'Oh, please!' Linda broke in. 'Is there any need to have another post-mortem on that wretched business? It happened. No one was to blame, as far as I can see; it was simply bad luck. You can't allow for every contingency.'

'That's what I mean,' Brady said. 'There has

24

to be a risk. Every time.'

'Not if you simply carry out your instructions,' Turner said, 'and don't go off on some wild goose chase of your own.'

'I have no intention of chasing wild geese. I wouldn't know what to do with the things if I caught them.'

'All right then. So we are to take it, are we, that you're willing to do this little job?'

There he goes, Brady thought, calling it a little job the same as Linda had done, as though it were no more than bathing the baby. Why did they always have to play the thing down? Why couldn't they be honest and say straight out: 'This is going to freeze your balls, Steve old son, but you're going to do it because we've got your head in a noose, and any nonsense from you, lad, and we knock the bolt out of the trap-door. So let's go, shall we? Let's go.' Little job, indeed!

'I'm not willing,' he said, 'but it's a shotgun wedding and I can't say no.'

'Come now,' Turner said deprecatingly, 'let's not talk about shotguns. I'm sure you don't imagine we'd try to twist your arm.'

'Wouldn't you?'

'Well, only if it was really necessary. Only if you left us no alternative. But you aren't going to do that, are you?'

'It wouldn't be any use, would it?'

'There, I knew you'd be sensible. You'll be travelling under an assumed name, of course.'

'Oh?'

'We think it hardly wise that you should go as Stephen Brady.'

'I don't think it's wise I should go at all.'

'Possibly not. But since you are going, we've decided to give you the name of Walter Storey.'

'Why?'

Turner raised his eyebrows inquiringly.

'I mean, why that name? Any particular reason?'

'Oh, I see. Well, yes, there is a reason. You are very similar in many respects to Mr Storey—age, background, education, physical appearance.'

'You mean there's a real one?'

'Oh, yes.'

'And how does he feel about this business?'

'He doesn't have any feelings about it. He doesn't know. At the present moment he's serving a term of imprisonment for obtaining money by false pretences.'

'You mean he's a con man?'

'Some people might call him that.'

'And while he's safely stowed away you borrow his passport. Is that it?'

'Why not? He's hardly likely to be using it for quite a while. It'll have your photograph and signature on it, of course. Your signature in the name of Walter Storey, I mean.'

'Is all this legal?'

Turner smiled blandly. 'Where the interests

26

of the realm are at stake all things are legal.'

Brady thought there might be more than one opinion on that score, but there seemed to be no point in arguing about it. He was not sure he much cared for taking on the identity of a con merchant, but at least he was never likely to come face to face with the real Walter Storey; which was perhaps as well.

'When do I leave?'

'Two weeks from today. We have a cabin reserved for you on board a ship called the "Baltic Swan".'

'You mean I'm travelling by sea?'

'Have you any objection?'

'I suppose not. If I've got to go, it makes very little difference what form of transport it is.'

'You will disembark at Gdansk, which I hardly need to tell you used to be Danzig and a bit of a shuttlecock between Poland and Germany, with spells as a free city. For the present it seems to be sitting well inside Poland and there's none of that nonsense regarding a Polish Corridor to the Baltic which caused so much trouble in the Thirties by cutting between East Prussia and the rest of Germany.'

'I did know that,' Brady said. 'You can skip the history lesson.'

Turner nodded. 'I'm glad to hear it. You might be surprised to learn how many of your generation are abysmally ignorant of such matters, which changed the course of Europe. Anyway, there's no Corridor to bother us these days, thank goodness; we've got enough troubles without that.'

'What do I do when I get to Gdansk?'

'You go to the Gizycko Hotel and book a room.'

'And then?'

'Then you wait for further instructions. You don't speak Polish, I suppose?'

'Not a word.'

'Well, it doesn't matter. Probably only make them suspicious if you did. You'll manage.'

'Don't I get any more information? Like what I'm going there for.'

'You don't need to know that. Yet. Just do as you're told.'

'So I'm to be in the dark? It's going to be a mystery tour?'

'Call it a blind date,' Turner said.

'I never did like blind dates. I always seemed to end up with a crow.'

'Maybe this time you'll be luckier.'

'I doubt it,' Brady said.

Before he left Turner opened a safe and took out a cash-box. From the box he counted out forty-five ten-pound notes.

'The first thing you'd better do is pay off that gambling debt. We don't want those goons to try beating you up again. Next time there might be no one to get you out of trouble and they might make a real job of it; put you out of action for a while.'

Brady took the money. 'And of course you've got a vested interest in me now, haven't you?'

'Precisely,' Turner said. 'And Miss Manning had better go with you.'

'To see that I do in fact hand over the cash? Don't you trust me?'

Turner scratched his cheek with the stem of the burnt-down pipe. 'Oh, I trust you, Brady. But I like to make sure my trust isn't misplaced, if you see what I mean.'

'I see what you mean,' Brady said. 'You mean you don't trust me.'

*　　*　　*

He sat in the Lotus while Linda Manning drove. He noticed that she drove very competently, but he had noticed that before—in other cars.

'It would be nice,' he said, 'if I didn't have to give this money to that swine Milligan. We could use it for much better purposes.'

'Like what, for instance?'

'Like maybe a holiday for two on the Costa Brava—or even Brighton.'

'A holiday for you and me?'

'That is rather what I had in mind.'

'Forget it, Steve; you've got a job to do.'

'But don't you think it would be nice?'

'Whether I do or do not makes no

difference. It just isn't on.'

Brady sighed. 'I suppose not. Don't give up thinking about it, though. When I come back I'll be in the money. Right?'

'There'll be some to come—if you've earned it.'

'If I ever get it I shall have earned it, that's for certain. So how about it then?'

'How about what then?'

'The holiday for two.'

'Don't you think it would be rather feckless to throw your capital away like that?'

'In my book it wouldn't be throwing it away.'

'No?'

'No. So how about it?'

'I think we'd better wait and see how things pan out.' He left it at that and contented himself with watching her drive for a while—which was a pleasant enough occupation on a sunny morning, even in the snarl of London's traffic. But five minutes later he had another bright idea. 'Why don't you come to Poland with me?'

'It's not on the programme.'

'It could be put on.'

'No, it couldn't.'

'Why not?'

'I can't explain that to you, Steve.'

'I'd feel a lot happier about going if you were with me.'

'Maybe you would.'

'You inspire me with confidence. Not to

mention a few other things.'

'Let's not go into that,' she said.

'You came with me to Russia.'

'No. You came with me.'

'Isn't that the same thing?'

'Not precisely. Anyway, this is quite a different sort of affair.'

'You don't have to tell me that,' Brady said.

They came to Milligan's place. It was closed at that hour of the day but they went round to the back. Milligan was there in his shirt-sleeves checking a delivery of liquor. He was a grossly fat man with a stone-bald head and a drooping moustache. He looked at Brady with a certain wariness, as though scenting trouble.

'What do you want?'

'I owe you some money,' Brady said.

'That's right.'

'I've come to pay you.'

Milligan relaxed. He relaxed enough to take a closer look at Linda Manning, and he seemed to like what he saw.

'Come into my office,' he said. 'The young lady is with you?'

'What does it look like?'

'It looks like she's with you. Some people, they have all the luck.' Milligan gave a leer.

'Shall we go into the office?' Linda said curtly.

Brady could see that she had not exactly taken to Milligan, and he was not surprised. If anybody wanted the truth, he had never taken

31

to Milligan himself. The fact that Milligan had sent a couple of thugs to beat him up had done nothing to sweeten his feelings towards the man. Indeed, it would have given him considerable pleasure to sink his fist into that fat paunch and watch the effect; but it would not have been wise. Turner for one would not have approved. Turner wanted him to stay out of trouble—at least until he had carried out his assignment.

'Certainly, certainly,' Milligan said. 'Come this way.' He turned and waddled on ahead of them, wheezing slightly like a man who smoked too much and breathed too little fresh air.

The office was cramped and stuffy. Milligan invited them to sit down but they preferred to stand.

'This won't take long,' Brady said. He hauled out the money Turner had given him and dropped it on the desk behind which Milligan had eased himself into a swivel chair. 'You'd better count it.'

Milligan looked at the money. 'You think I need to do that? You think I'm afraid you'd try to cheat me?'

'You mean you aren't?'

'Why should I be? I know you're honest.'

'Is that why you set your gorillas on to me?'

'Gorillas!'

'Your two strong-arm boys—Harry and Joe.'

'They've been molesting you?' Milligan

sounded shocked.

'Now don't tell me you didn't know. Don't tell me they weren't acting on your orders.'

Milligan shook his head. 'Oh, no, no. I may have mentioned in their hearing that you owed me a small sum of money and that you were being a little slow in paying. I may even have asked if they could persuade you to cough up. But I never dreamed they would resort to violence; believe me, nothing was further from my mind. I thought they would just talk to you.'

'You're a rotten liar,' Brady said.

'Now, now, no harsh words.' Milligan reached out for the notes and started counting them in an absent-minded sort of way, so it looked as though he was like Turner: he believed in making sure his trust was not misplaced. 'Yes,' he said when he had completed the counting. 'Four hundred and fifty pounds. So now we are all square.'

'When you've given me my cheque.'

'Ah, of course.' Milligan unlocked a safe, found the cheque and handed it to Brady. 'You know you're welcome to come to the club any time you wish to try your luck.'

'He won't be trying his luck again,' Linda said.

Milligan glanced at her and then at the money. 'So that's the way it is.'

Brady felt he could read what was in the fat man's mind. Milligan believed that Linda had paid the gaming debt on condition that he stayed away from the tables in future. It was probably the impression she had intended giving.

'And now,' she said, 'there seems to be nothing more to do here, so I think we may as well go. Are you ready, Steve?'

'I'm ready,' Brady said.

As he followed her out of the office the grin on Milligan's face made him once again feel strongly inclined to indulge in a little physical violence, but he resisted the temptation.

'Be seeing you,' Milligan said; and he began to laugh wheezily.

Brady hoped he would choke himself.

CHAPTER THREE

TAIL

'It's no trouble at all,' Braddock said. 'I've got nothing in particular to do, apart from the usual duties on board ship while we're in port. And I've been to Gdansk before, so it's nothing new to me. This is our regular run, you know.'

Brady was glad enough to accept Braddock's offer of help. Eric Braddock was second mate of the 'Baltic Swan', which was a cargo ship with accommodation for a handful of passengers, and he had introduced himself to Brady on the first day of the voyage. Brady wondered whether this was altogether fortuitous or whether Braddock was perhaps working for Turner's department on the side. There was no solid reason for supposing that he was but you could never be sure about such things, and he had certainly been very helpful. He was about the same age as Brady, a likeable ginger-haired man with a snub nose and a good coating of freckles.

'You might have a bit of difficulty finding the hotel on your own, seeing that you're a stranger to the town and don't speak Polish.'

Brady agreed that this was likely. He could see a lot of difficulties looming up ahead and was no more happy about this assignment now than he had been at the start. A shade less so, if anything.

The ship had sailed from Hull and Linda Manning had driven him up from London in her Lotus. He had had a few meetings with her in the preceding fortnight and she had brought the doctored passport belonging to Walter Storey, which was complete with Polish visa.

'So our friend Walter intended paying a visit to Poland.'

Linda had merely smiled enigmatically and he had not pursued the matter any further. He was not at all sure he wanted to know whether the visa was genuine or not; either way he had to rely on it to get him through.

In the event it all went smoothly enough; the Polish officials seemed friendly enough and appeared to take him at face value. He gave the purpose of his visit as 'cultural', which sounded impressive and was sufficiently vague to cover a pretty wide field of activity—a trip to Warsaw or Krakow, a journey through the countryside, anything. Not that he had any intention of looking for culture, but the fact was he had no idea what he was going to do beyond checking in at the Gizycko Hotel; from there he had to take things as they came. Fortunately it appeared that the Polish authorities had no objection to tourists wandering around on their own if that was the way they wanted it; you could have a conducted tour if you wished but it was not forced on you.

'They're fairly relaxed these days,' Braddock told him. 'This may be a Communist country but the people have managed to take a lot of the rough edges off the strict Party doctrine. To a large extent they've made it work their way. And another thing, the Catholic Church is still a powerful influence; the Government have never been able to suppress it, hard as they've tried, and they seem to have resigned themselves to a compromise.'

Braddock managed to obtain a taxi. It was driven by a cheerful, obliging man whose grin revealed a few gaps in his teeth. Brady had only one suitcase; Linda had advised him to keep his luggage to a minimum and he had never made it a practice to clutter himself with a lot of unnecessary gear when travelling.

'It's quite a way into town,' Braddock said. 'It'll take a bit of time.'

'I'm in no hurry,' Brady said.

For the first part it was dockland, ship-building yards, factories, distilleries, the usual unsightly clutter of an industrial society, utilitarian and basically unattractive. Later, when they came to the old city, it was different; there were narrow cobbled streets and squares, gabled houses scarcely changed since mediaeval times, a sense of history, the Hanseatic League, Teutonic knights, Prussian armies, Nazi tanks . . .

'It took a pasting in the last war,' Braddock said. 'It's a wonder any of the old buildings were left. They've done a lot of rebuilding in the old style. Great ones for that kind of thing, the Poles; look what they've done in Warsaw. Of course they've had plenty of experience of making things rise again from the ashes, all through the ages. They've been overrun time after time; always had invaders bringing death and destruction—Germans, Russians, the lot. But they've always pulled themselves up off the floor, built it all again. Resilient, that's what they are.'

'I get the impression you like them,' Brady said.

'I do. What's more, I admire them. Look at Poland. Look at it on the map. It's just one big flat open country in the middle of Europe, with a few mountains in the south but no natural defences at all to east or west. Yet they fight; they fight even when it's hopeless, even when the enemies come in from both sides at once, like last time, and their so-called friends are a thousand miles away and not lifting a finger to help.'

'There was no way of helping.'

'True,' Braddock admitted. 'We gave them a guarantee and it wasn't worth a can of warm spit, not when the chips were down.'

The Gizycko Hotel was modest and unimposing; it was situated in a modest, unimposing street; it was the kind of place

38

a person might choose if he wanted decent accommodation at a reasonable price; something neither luxurious nor seedy, quiet and discreet.

'You'll be comfortable here,' Braddock said.

Brady did not ask him how he knew. Possibly he had stayed at the Gizycko himself.

He went in with Brady. 'Just in case there's no one around who speaks English.'

In fact there had been no need to worry on that score: the girl at the reception desk spoke passable English. She had flaxen hair, a plump face of no great beauty and a friendly smile. Brady could remember having cooler welcomes in hotels on the other side of the Iron Curtain.

'Yes, Mr Storey, we can let you have a room. You wish to stay long?'

'No,' Brady said, 'not long. One or two nights perhaps. That will be all right?'

'Of course.'

The room was on the second floor. Braddock, still solicitous for his welfare, went up with him and had a look at it. There was nothing to complain about; it was an austere rectangular box with cream-coloured walls and a window looking out on to the street; the furnishing was all that was essential and nothing that was not. It appeared clean and hygienic, like a private room in a hospital.

'All right?' Braddock asked.

'It'll do. It'll do fine.'

'Any further help you need?'

Brady thought there might well be a lot of further help he needed, but he doubted whether that was the kind of help Braddock meant.

'Nothing, thanks. It's good of you to have taken so much bother.'

'No bother,' Braddock said. 'Only too glad to lend a hand. Know what it's like to be in a strange country without friends.'

He left soon after that. Brady still could not be sure whether he had been doing a job of work or had merely been going through the Boy Scout routine. Either way, he did not expect to see any more of Braddock unless he returned to England on board the 'Baltic Swan'. But before he could even think about returning he had to do whatever it was he had been sent to Poland to do. And what that was he would not find out until the blind date turned up. He had to admit that things had gone pretty smoothly so far, but he was not kidding himself they would continue to do so; somewhere along the line there was bound to be a joker waiting to dish out a bit of nastiness; he had never been more certain of anything in his life.

He took a few things out of the suitcase and after he had done that he walked over to the window and watched the traffic going past in the street. He got tired of that after a while; he was not really a traffic-watcher by nature. He

40

looked at his watch; the hands pointed to three-twenty-five; there was a lot of day still to be got through. He decided to go for a walk and take a look at Gdansk. If anyone came to see him they would have to wait or call again.

When he left the hotel he found that the sky, which had been clear during the earlier part of the day, had become overcast. There was a certain oppressiveness in the air, a threat of rain perhaps, though for the present it was dry. He had been walking for some fifteen minutes when the feeling grew upon him that he was being followed. There was a man about twenty yards behind whom he felt sure he had noticed lounging on the pavement when he had looked out of the window of his room. He had seen the man again on leaving the hotel but had thought nothing of it. Now, however, he could hardly dismiss as a coincidence the fact that the lounger should still be only a few paces away from him.

He stopped and gazed into a shop window. From the corner of his eye he saw that the man had also stopped and was gazing into another shop window. The fellow had a long thin face like an emaciated goat and his black hair was receding from his forehead; he was wearing a greasy jacket and black trousers; he did not look prosperous.

After a minute or two Brady walked on again. The man did the same. Brady stopped at another shop window. The man stopped also. Brady crossed to the opposite side of the street. A few seconds later the man was on that side, too.

Brady could no longer be in any doubt that the man was on his tail. But why? Was he a police spy and was he, Brady, already under surveillance so soon after planting his feet on Polish soil? It very much looked like it. Maybe that passport to which he had no right had not been accepted at its face value after all; maybe the irregularity had been reported and this was the result.

Yet if the man in the greasy jacket was indeed a tail, he was a singularly clumsy one; he was making scarcely any attempt to disguise his purpose. Though perhaps that was not because of any lack of skill but because he simply did not care whether he was detected or not; perhaps it was merely an indication of the contempt with which he regarded the person he was tailing.

Brady did not like it. It is not, even in the best of circumstances, particularly pleasant to discover that one's footsteps are being dogged by a perfect stranger; the most disturbing conclusions are liable to force their way into the mind. The present circumstances were certainly not of the best and Brady found the attentions of the man in the greasy jacket rather more than merely disturbing; he found them downright frightening, and the plain fact of the matter was that he was dead scared. He had been expecting things to go wrong, because in his experience that was the way they usually did go, but he had been counting on a little more time than this; he had not imagined he would be picked up quite so quickly. If this was the way it started, how in hell was it going to finish?

He found himself walking rather faster. It made no difference; the follower kept pace, not allowing the gap between the two of them to widen by any appreciable amount. Then a crush of people spilling out of a bus got in the way and Brady was forced almost to a standstill. He was in the process of forcing a path through the jostling crowd when he suddenly found the man in the greasy jacket close beside him. For a moment he gazed into the man's eyes, which were a dull slaty colour and utterly lacking in warmth; then a movement of people behind thrust him hard up against the greasy jacket and he felt a hand groping for his breast pocket.

He knew then that he had been wrong in his deduction; the man had not been following him under orders from any department of state security as he had feared; the purpose behind the operation was a far more mundane one and the fellow was in fact nothing more than a common pickpocket who was interested only in the possibility of snatching a wallet.

'Damn you,' Brady muttered; and he made a grab at the man's wrist but could not hold on. The man tore himself free, turned and was gone, worming a way through the press and darting off down a side-street.

Brady thought of giving chase and abandoned the idea instantly. No one but himself appeared to have noticed what had occurred and the last thing he desired was to attract attention to himself. Moreover, the pickpocket had taken nothing; Brady had been too quick to spot his purpose and the hand thrust inside his coat had come out empty. The incident had given him a few unpleasant moments but the final sensation was one of relief at the realisation that he was not after all under surveillance. He did not even feel any strong resentment against the singularly inept pickpocket who must surely get a poor sort of living at the game if he was no more skilful than this.

It was not until Brady had returned to his room at the hotel that he was forced to alter his opinion of the skill of the man in the greasy jacket and to give him credit for being rather less inept than he had supposed. Chancing to put a hand in one of the outer pockets of his own jacket he discovered a piece of paper that had certainly not been there earlier. The obvious deduction was that the supposed pick-pocket, while making a diversionary dip with one hand, had at the same moment slipped the paper into another pocket with his other hand.

The paper was folded twice. Brady opened

it out and read the brief message written on it in block lettering: 'Go to the Zoppotski Theatre tonight.'

He read it twice, then went to the bathroom, tore the paper into small pieces and flushed them down the lavatory. Having completed this disposal job he descended the stairs to the lobby and asked the girl at the reception desk whether she could recommend some place of entertainment for the evening. She seemed only too pleased to help and had soon given him a list of establishments which she could personally assure him were above reproach. The Zoppotski was not one of them and Brady saw that he would have to be a little more specific.

'I have been told the Zoppotski Theatre is very good.'

'The Zoppotski!' She seemed surprised, possibly a shade disapproving also. 'I am not sure you would like it there. It is popular with students—'

'Do you object to students?'

'No, it is not that. But it is not quite—well—respectable. It is—'

'I think I should like to visit a theatre that is not quite respectable,' Brady said.

There was certainly disapproval in the way she looked at him now. He had a feeling that he had gone down in her estimation. 'Well, if that is your wish—'

'It is my wish. Could you tell me how to

45

get there?'

'It is not easy to find. You had better take a taxi. Would you like me to order one for you?'

Brady thought about it. 'Do you know what time the performance begins ?'

'Oh,' she said, 'there is no need to bother about that. It is not that kind of theatre. You can go any time.'

It began to sound like a strip joint, but were there such places in Communist countries? If so they were certainly becoming more tolerant. Or would permissive be the word?

'Shall we say eight o'clock then?'

She gave a faint shrug as though repudiating any further responsibility in the matter; if he insisted on going to the Zoppotski against her advice that was his affair; he had been warned.

'As you wish, Mr Storey.'

CHAPTER FOUR

CLOAK AND DAGGER LARK

The taxi arrived at the hotel dead on time. The driver, a man well past middle age and with a heavily creased face like an ageing bloodhound, possessed a few words of English which he appeared delighted to use. Sure he knew the Zoppotski; he sometimes went there himself; it was a damn good show. He did not look like a student, so evidently the Zoppotski had others on its list of patrons, even taxi-drivers.

Brady got into the taxi and allowed himself to be driven away to this rendezvous of which he knew nothing and where he would supposedly make some kind of contact. Always supposing the note had been genuine. Yet how could it be anything else? Who would slip such a message into his pocket just for the fun of the thing? As a method of advertising the theatre it would have been too bizarre to be credible. Yes, it had certainly been genuine, even if a trifle melodramatic, no doubt about that.

Nevertheless, he still felt uneasy; he was like a pawn being moved around the board by forces he did not understand and over which he had no control. And was it not all in the game for a pawn to be sacrificed if such a move were calculated to win an ultimate advantage? Suppose he had been sent out as a sacrifice in order to assist some devious plan concocted in Turner's mind or in the minds of those shadowy figures in the background who were Turner's superiors and whom he, Brady, had never seen. He would not have put it past them; he felt pretty certain Turner would not have hesitated to throw him to the wolves if it had seemed necessary or even expedient to do so. And Linda? Would she be as ruthless? No, he did not believe that of her. But she might not know; they didn't tell her everything, did they?

By the time he had thought all this out he was so much on edge he was ready to stop the taxi and tell the driver to take him back to the hotel. But he did nothing; he let himself be carried along like a piece of flotsam drifting with the tide. It had all become somehow inevitable—whatever it might be.

It was growing dark and the rain that had been threatening since early afternoon had at last begun to fall. Under the light of the street-lamps the wet paving glistened metallically. The engine of the taxi was making a lot of noise, as though it could have done with an overhaul. The hair at the back of the driver's neck was cropped short and there were horizontal creases in the neck. Brady felt envious of this man; at least he knew where he was going.

The entrance was in an alleyway which was so narrow it was impossible for the taxi to get into it; the alleyway was strictly for pedestrians only. The driver stopped and opened the door for Brady to get out.

'From here is walk.' He pointed down the alleyway. 'Just short way. You see light?'

Brady could see the light; it was red; it seemed appropriate. He paid the driver and walked towards it in the falling rain. He heard the taxi drive away; he was on his own again. And he was free to make a choice; he could go to the theatre or he could walk straight past, give it a miss. But where would be the sense in that? He had come to Gdansk to do a job and he had better get on with it. Besides, who wanted to walk around in the rain? Not Steve Brady.

The entrance to the Zoppotski was a nice blend of the garish and the seedy. It looked old; in the early days of the film industry there had been a lot of little flea-pit cinemas with the same kind of appearance: naked electric light bulbs, flaking paint, tarnished gilt, frames of photographs giving a promise of what might be seen within, an indefinable odour of God knew what . . .

Brady pushed open a glass door and there was a bit of tiled foyer with a pay-desk on the right. He could see no one on duty at the pay-desk, but as he approached it a head popped up and a small woman with large glasses and a lot of large beads festooned about her neck like Hawaiian garlands stared at him in stony silence.

Brady could see no list of seat prices and in answer to a question put to her in English the woman merely answered with a flood of words which were incomprehensible to him and were presumably Polish. He gathered from this that she did not understand English and he decided that it would be best to try some money; people were always saying that money talked, though he personally had never heard any of the stuff utter a damned word, and maybe Polish money would talk Polish. He took a one-hundred-zloty note from his wallet and laid it on the pay-desk. It worked; the woman picked it up, tore a ticket off a roll and handed it to him with a handful of change.

There seemed to be only one doorway which could possibly give access to the auditorium and Brady walked towards it. The woman watched him as she might have watched someone she suspected of having come to rob the till. There were two swing doors which had taken a lot of hard wear in their time; they creaked slightly as he made his way through and as soon as he came out on the other side he knew what the receptionist at the hotel had meant when she had told him it was not quite respectable. It had the appearance of a somewhat down-at-heel cabaret. The light was rather dim and there were tables dotted around the floor, while at one end of the room was a low, bare stage with a brick wall at the back and no curtain. Nothing in the way of entertainment was going on at that moment, but there was an upright piano just off the stage on the left and a thin young man with lank hair was sitting on the stool and drinking from a mug of beer.

Brady stood just inside the doorway taking a good look at the place. He would have said it was true about students patronising the Zoppotski; there were a lot of young people, male and female, who seemed the student type. But there were others too, more in the mould of the taxi-driver. A buzz of animated conversation rose from the tables; the air was impregnated with tobacco smoke and the odour of food and drink; he got an impression of gaiety, of high spirits, of people enjoying themselves.

Most of the tables were already occupied, but he spotted a vacant one pushed up against the wall not far from the piano and quite close to the stage. He made his way to it and sat down with his back to the wall. He could see why no one had been sitting there: because of its situation the view of the stage was partly blocked by the piano. He was not worried about that; he had not really come to see the show; he was not sure what he had come for but it was certainly not for that.

A man in shirt-sleeves and a white apron who was obviously a waiter came over to the table, said something and waited expectantly. Brady gathered that he was asking for an order. He was not hungry; he had eaten at the hotel before leaving and was not ready for another meal. He decided to settle for a drink. But not vodka; Turner had warned him about that. 'They make vodkas up to seventy degrees over proof; that's ninety-seven per cent alcohol. Poison.' Brady had asked him how he knew that if he had never been to Poland and he had said that he had his sources of information. Brady decided to trust Turner's sources of information and stay off vodka; he had never cared much for the stuff anyway and this was no time to get stewed to the eyeballs.

'Beer,' he said. He pointed to the mug in the pianist's hand and held up one finger. 'One beer.'

The waiter got on to it fairly quickly; he went away and came back with a mug of pale frothy beer which looked like a pint but was probably half a litre. Brady put some money on the table and let the waiter take what he wanted.

The pianist suddenly started knocking hell out of the keys and a pair of clowns popped on to the stage and went through a routine. Brady watched as much as came into his line of sight and decided there was not a lot to it unless the dialogue had some point he was missing. The act was certainly going down well enough with the rest of the audience, who were giving it all their attention and laughing like mad. It had to be the dialogue.

A sketch followed. The props consisted of a plain wooden table, a couple of chairs and a telephone. He felt pretty sure this was satire, and maybe political satire at that. He saw that he had been wrong in thinking the Zoppotski might be a strip joint, so maybe its decadence took another form. He could not be sure, of course; without understanding the language he could not be certain what it was all about, but whatever it was, it was getting across to the audience; they were lapping it up and loving it. Brady, sipping his beer in solitary silence, had a feeling of being odd man out, a kind of skeleton at the feast.

The sketch was followed by a stand-up comic in a tophat, and Brady was beginning to yawn. Nobody had shown any inclination to make contact with him and he thought it was about time something happened. He had played his part, so how about some action from the opposite number.

Then a girl walked on to the stage and sang a song and he forgot about yawning. He had a good view of her because she came right up to the front of the boards and that brought her clear of the piano. He was rather glad about that; he would have been sorry not to see her clearly, since she was undoubtedly worth looking at. She was quite plainly dressed in a black skirt and a white blouse with long sleeves and a polo neck; no jewellery of any kind, not a brooch nor a bracelet nor an earring, nothing whatever to lessen the severe simplicity of the ensemble; even her shoes were black and low-heeled. She had blonde hair, fringed across the forehead and coming smoothly down on each side of her face to a sudden inward curve at the level of the chin. She looked young and demure and oddly vulnerable, and perhaps it was only the youth that was genuine—that and the enchanting loveliness of her. For she was indeed enchanting and indeed lovely. Brady had been feeling bored with the show, but not now, not any more, he even forgot to drink his beer.

Her singing put him in mind of lots of things which might have had nothing whatever to do with the song. It had a strangely captivating quality and yet was hardly singing at all in the strictest sense; she would never have made a name for herself in opera. But perhaps she had never had any ambitions in that direction; perhaps this was all she wanted. And she had her audience; they were silent now, loving her; all the men at least; maybe thinking what it would be like to wake up with her head beside them on the pillow. Brady was having some thoughts along those lines himself.

When the first song was finished she sang another and then a third, with the piano jangling out an accompaniment, but not too loudly, because nobody was there to hear the thin young man do his piece; he was just part of the trimming. They wanted more from her, but they had had their ration and she gave a bow and walked off into the wings, and they could shout for her as much as they liked, she was not coming back. A juggler came on and went through his act with an air of quiet desperation, as if he knew he was not welcome; it was a difficult spot on the programme, following the blonde girl. He was a good juggler, but it made no difference.

Brady had almost finished his beer when a curtain on the other side of the piano was pulled aside and the girl appeared. She walked past the pianist and came up to Brady's table, and sat down on a spare chair, facing him.

'You don't mind?' she said, and she said it in English, which surprised him.

He was certainly not going to raise any objection, but it did occur to him that things might be a shade awkward if his contact turned up and found him sitting with a blonde. Well, if so it was just too bad; the man should have shown himself earlier; now he could do the waiting.

'No,' he said, 'I don't mind. Why should I?'

She looked just as young as she had on the stage and there was not a trace of make-up on her face that he could detect. Not that she needed any; she was just about perfect as she

55

was to his way of thinking.

'You had better buy me a drink,' she said. 'It will seem more natural.'

Without waiting for him to agree or object she signalled to the waiter and gave the order, and she must have ordered another beer for him, too, because when the waiter returned there was a full mug on the tray as well as a small glass of something which might have been wine for her.

Brady paid. Why not? It was not his money.

The waiter went away and she picked up her glass, looking at him over the rim. 'To you, Mr Storey,' she said. Brady was startled. 'You know my name!'

'Naturally. I am your contact.'

'You!'

'Please don't look so surprised,' she said. 'Try to look as though life is being rather good to you, even if you don't feel it is.'

Brady grinned at her. 'Oh, I feel it is; at this moment I certainly feel that. But I'm bound to be surprised; you're not at all what I was expecting.'

'And what exactly were you expecting? A furtive little man in a shabby raincoat perhaps?'

'Perhaps.'

'Would you have preferred that?'

'Now you're joking, of course. Do I get to know your name?'

'Don't you know it already?'

'How should I?'

'It's on the programme.'

'I haven't seen a programme.'

'I am Paula Nowicki.'

'It's a nice name,' Brady said. 'And I liked the act.'

She made a small gesture as though dismissing something of no importance. 'Let us not talk about that. There is another matter.'

'You'd better tell me about it. I'm still in the dark.'

It occurred to him that he ought to ask her for some proof that she was genuine. But what proof could she have given? There had been no prearranged plan for an exchange of secret passwords or anything of that kind; Turner had been a trifle lax in that respect, Brady thought; instructions had been of the barest and simplest description: Go to Gdansk and wait for the contact. He had not even been told that the contact would be a girl. Maybe Turner had not known that, either.

It was possible that she guessed what was passing in his mind, for she said: 'You are wondering perhaps whether you can trust me. Am I in fact what I pretend to be or am I leading you into a trap?'

Brady said nothing. The girl sipped her wine and treated him to a cool appraisal with a pair of very intelligent blue eyes.

'But the fact is, Mr Storey, that you have no choice. You have to trust me, don't you? What else can you do? Go home and tell your people you didn't like the look of me?'

'That wouldn't be the truth,' Brady said. 'There may be some parts of the deal I don't like, but the look of you isn't one of them. And since it seems that we're going to be working together for a time at least, don't you think it would make it a bit less formal if you called me Walter?'

It had been on the tip of his tongue to say 'Steve'; the 'Walter' came out with a certain hesitancy; it was not a name he would have chosen for himself, but he had had no say in the matter and he was stuck with it now.

'Very well,' she said, 'if it pleases you— Walter. Now shall we get down to business?'

'If it pleases you—Paula.'

She gave a momentary frown, as though she disapproved of the levity in his tone. It was, after all, a serious matter and not a subject for banter.

'You are to leave Gdansk tomorrow.'

'Oh! And where am I to go?'

'There is no need for you to know that— yet.'

'You mean somebody is coming along to tell me later?'

She gave a sigh which might have been expressing exasperation. 'Don't you understand? I am to be your guide. I shall go with you.'

Brady's spirits rose. 'That sounds a lot

better. Yes, I like the sound of that. Are you going to call for me at the Gizycko Hotel?'

'No; that would not be wise, I think. You will pay your bill and check out at half-past nine; the time is important, so do not be late. Outside the hotel you will turn to the left and walk down the street until you come to the second cross-roads; there you will turn right and continue walking.'

'Don't forget I shall be carrying my luggage,' Brady said. He was not sure he liked the idea of all that walking with a suitcase.

'How much luggage?' the girl asked.

He told her.

'Surely that is not too much to carry.'

'It depends how far I have to carry it.'

'It will not be far. But be sure not to be late.'

'Suppose I don't see you. Do I just go on walking?'

'You will see me. But in any case don't go further than the baker's shop.'

'What baker's shop?'

'You can't miss it. There's a sign like a loaf of bread over the door.'

He was still not at all sure he liked it very much. And could he really trust her?

'You're very young for this kind of thing,' he said.

'What kind of thing?'

'Well, you know—the cloak and dagger lark.'

Her brow furrowed slightly. 'I don't think

59

I've ever heard that expression—'

'No? Well, it doesn't matter. But you're still too young.'

'Maybe not quite as young as you imagine.'

'You'll surprise me if you say you're more than twenty.'

'Very well then,' she said, 'I'll surprise you. I'm twenty-two.'

'Is that the truth?'

'Why should I lie about it?'

'No reason at all. But I'd have guessed nineteen.'

'It would have been a bad guess. Now let me try. You're thirty. Am I near?'

'Near enough,' Brady said. And he felt suddenly old. She left him soon after that. 'It is best I don't stay talking with you too long. Wait a while and then go back to your hotel. I will see you tomorrow.'

He watched her until she had vanished behind the curtain on the other side of the piano. He thought about hanging on in the hope of seeing her on stage again but decided it was best to do as she had advised. He could wait until tomorrow. He just hoped she turned up, that was all—and not only because of the job, either.

It was still raining when he left the Zoppotski and he had some difficulty in finding a taxi to take him back to the hotel. When he eventually got there he was feeling damp and depressed. He retired to bed at once and dreamed of a lot of unpleasant things happening to him. He had no need of any Joseph to tell him what this meant: it meant he was expecting a lot of unpleasant things to happen to him.

He had known that already.

CHAPTER FIVE

JOURNEY WITH PAULA

The plump girl with the flaxen hair who had been so friendly when he checked in at the Gizycko Hotel seemed rather less friendly now that he was checking out. She had in fact grown markedly cooler towards him from the moment when he had ignored her advice and had insisted on going to the Zoppotski Theatre.

'You are leaving so soon, Mr Storey?'

'Yes.'

'Was the room not satisfactory?'

'The room was perfectly satisfactory. I told you I might not be needing it for more than one night.'

'You have decided to leave Gdansk, perhaps?'

Brady felt like telling her it was none of her business whether he left Gdansk or not, but he decided not to. She seemed very inquisitive, he thought; possibly even a trifle suspicious? No; that was nonsense; why on earth should she be suspicious? He was imagining things.

'Perhaps,' he said.

'You do not like the town?'

'I think it's a very nice town. But my time is limited.'

'Ah,' she said, and again he had that impression of suspicion, unmistakably. As though to have limited time were in itself evidence of illegal activities.

He paid the bill and picked up his suitcase.

'Do you wish me to call a taxi for you, Mr Storey?'

'No,' he said. 'It's a pleasant morning. I'll walk.'

She glanced at the suitcase. He knew it sounded crazy. Where was he going to walk to? He felt impelled to offer a bit more information.

'I'll catch a bus or something.'

'Just as you wish, Mr Storey.' Her mouth closed primly and she seemed to be dismissing him with a certain contempt. She had done her best to help him but he had insisted on going his own way. Very well, if that was the way he wanted it . . .

He was aware of her gaze fixed upon him as he left the hotel, and he was glad to let the door close behind him and to get beyond the range of her disapproving eyes. He turned left and began to walk. It was not yet half-past nine; there could be no complaint regarding his punctuality.

The rain had stopped during the night, but there was a cool wind blowing along the street and he was heading into it. With the suitcase in his hand he felt like a door-to-door salesman. He reached the first cross-roads and went past it and came to the second. There was a lot of traffic—cars, lorries puffing out diesel exhaust, bicycles. He turned to the right as Paula Nowicki had instructed him and went on his way.

He was keeping a sharp lookout for the girl, but there was no one among the hurrying pedestrians who looked at all like her. Perhaps she would pick him up in a car; and he rather hoped she would, because the suitcase was beginning to feel as if it contained a roll of lead stolen from a church roof. It was turning into a pretty long walk, whatever she might have said about its not being far, and then he spotted the baker's shop, and she had been right about that—he couldn't miss it; not with that slab of wood carved in the shape of a loaf of bread hanging like an inn sign over the doorway.

He came to a halt. She had told him not to go any further than that, and he had better not. But she had still not put in an appearance and he was feeling a bit peeved; if he had made a point of being on time she ought to have had the decency to do so as well. Now what should he do? Hang around outside the baker's shop? Go in and buy a loaf? Start walking back the way he had come? He was feeling edgy besides being peeved; he was sure the suitcase was making him conspicuous, and though nobody appeared to be taking any particular notice of him there was no telling that he might not be under observation. And suppose the girl failed to arrive at all—what then? Go back to the Gizycko Hotel and say he had changed his mind and would like his room for another night? That would certainly make the plump girl's eyes pop. And then pay another visit to the Zoppotski Theatre and try to contact Paula Nowicki there? Or just say to hell with the whole rotten business and take the next ship or plane back to England?

That final alternative had considerable attraction. After all, what could Turner do? The gambling debt was paid and they would have a job to get the money back from him now. But might they not send him out to Poland again—under duress—and tell him to see the job through and not play any more monkey tricks? It was possible; it was even probable. So maybe he had better make a few more efforts before throwing in his hand; maybe he had better hang on a while longer and hope that things would work out.

The window of the baker's shop attracted his attention. He put the suitcase down and stared at the shelves of cakes and pastries and various kinds of bread, and the delectable odour that always went with bakeries drifted out to the pavement and set his nose twitching. He could see into the shop and there was a fat woman serving behind a counter. Suddenly she turned her head and saw him watching her; he was faintly embarrassed and quickly shifted his gaze away. He was about to pick up his suitcase and walk away from the window when he felt a touch on his arm. He had not been expecting it and was so startled that he made an involuntary backward movement as he swung round to see who it was who had touched him.

It was Paula Nowicki.

'Well,' she said, 'you are nervous. Did I frighten you?'

'I was beginning to think you weren't coming,' Brady said. 'I'd just about given you up.'

She glanced at the watch on her wrist. 'But it's only a little after half-past nine. You must have left the hotel rather early.'

She was right, of course; he had been getting into a lather over nothing. She was wearing a blue belted raincoat and a little hat of the same material perched on the back of her head, and she looked quite charming. There was a brown leather bag with a long strap slung over her left shoulder; it was rather big for a handbag and rather small for a suitcase, somewhere between the two. He wondered what she was carrying in it.

'We'd better go,' she said. 'We haven't a lot of time.'

He was reflecting that she looked just as good in daylight as she had looked sitting at his table the previous evening in the subdued lighting of the Zoppotski Theatre. He would have been happy to see her even if he had not needed her as a guide; he would have been happy to see a girl like her any time, anywhere.

He picked up the suitcase. 'I'm ready if you are. I'm just hoping we don't have to walk all the way.'

'I can promise you that,' she said.

It was in fact only a very short distance. It was a bus-stop and they had five minutes to wait before the bus came. They climbed on board with half a dozen other passengers and found a seat near the back. Paula bought the tickets and handed one to him.

'I suppose you wouldn't care to tell me where we're going now?' Brady said.

'Of course not,' she said. 'It's no secret. We're going to catch a train.'

*　　　*　　　*

There was something about railway stations that never failed to give Brady a feeling of excitement. However grimy or dilapidated they might be, there was a certain romantic aspect about them which somehow no airport had ever succeeded in reproducing. Not for him at any rate. When the station happened to be in a foreign country the effect was increased; when it was in a country on the wrong side of the Iron Curtain the excitement tended to have more than a dash of apprehension mixed in.

On the station in Gdansk he left all

arrangements to Paula Nowicki; he was in her hands now, and with a sense of fatalism he had decided to trust himself entirely to her. There was, after all, not much else he could do. The sight of a couple of armed policemen set his pulse racing, but the policemen were not showing any interest in him and the girl seemed unconcerned. He tried to reflect her nonchalance but found it difficult to do so while feeling like an escaped criminal with all the forces of law and order lined up against him.

When they were sitting in the train and waiting for it to start his nervousness increased. He was only too well aware of the fact that he was travelling with a passport to which he had no legal right, and that was a crime in any country. He even began to envy the real Walter Storey who was comfortably tucked away in a British gaol; you could hardly find anywhere safer than that.

'I do wish you would relax,' Paula said. 'Do you really want to attract attention?'

Brady looked at her. There was no hint of tension about her. Cool, that was what she was; cool. 'I don't know how you manage it.'

'Manage what?'

'To stay so calm. Aren't your nerves jangling?'

'Why should they be? There's nothing to worry about.'

'You mean it's all in the mind?'

'It's all in your mind.'

'Well, maybe it is. But I wish this train would get moving. What's keeping it?'

'It isn't due to leave for another five minutes. You must have patience.'

He tried to have patience. He also tried to relax. He thought of methods of relaxation he had read about in magazines or books or wherever, but none of them seemed suitable in the present circumstances. If he started going through deep-breathing rhythms or took up a yoga pose on the seat he was likely to attract far more notice in the crowded carriage than any amount of inner tension could possibly bring him. He gazed out of the window and caught sight of the two policemen again. Or another two. The place seemed to be crawling with cops.

Five minutes later, with a slight jolt, the train started moving.

'You see,' Paula said, a shade complacently, he thought, 'there was no need to be so bothered.'

'So three cheers for the Polish State Railways.'

'I think you are not in a very good mood, Walter.'

'Perhaps not. And perhaps now you'd like to tell me where this train is taking us.'

'To Torun.'

'How far is that?'

'About one hundred and fifty kilometres by

69

train.'

'And when we get there?'

'Suppose we just wait and see.'

'I seem to do a lot of that,' Brady said. 'And incidentally, what about the Zoppotski?'

'How do you mean—what about it?'

'I mean shouldn't you be performing there tonight? You'll never be back in time for that, will you?'

'And if I'm not?'

'Well, won't they fire you?'

'I don't think so. And I'm not very bothered if they do. I can find another job.'

He believed her. With her kind of talent she was not likely to find much difficulty in that respect. He was even a little surprised that she should have been performing in a dump like that.

The train dragged its way out of the environs of Gdansk and into the flat, open countryside of the North European plain, through which the Vistula flowed towards the Baltic. There were cultivated fields, pine forests, patches of marshland, villages, men driving tractors or horses, great flocks of geese; a vast panorama sliding past the windows. Brady glanced at the girl sitting beside him and saw that her face was averted. He wondered what was passing through her mind and he wondered why she was doing this kind of work. For the money? Or for some other reason? Maybe he would ask her sometime, if a suitable occasion arose. And maybe she would tell him. And again maybe she would not.

'What are you thinking about?' he asked.

His voice seemed to startle her, to bring her back from a great distance. She turned her head and looked at him, and he thought again how lovely she was.

'Many things,' she said. 'Many, many things.'

'Things in which I have no part?'

'Perhaps.'

He had a sense of being excluded, shut out. Yet how could it have been otherwise? He knew nothing of her life, her background; all those twenty-two years of hers had been passed without his even knowing of her existence—or she of his. They had come together briefly now by a mere chance, and he was nothing to her, no more than a piece of merchandise which she must transport from one place to another. He felt a touch of regret that it should be so, but that was the way it was.

'It's a pity,' he said. 'A great pity.'

'What is?'

'That things aren't different.'

She did not ask him what he meant by this, but perhaps she understood. And maybe she looked a little regretful too. Or was he imagining that?

*   *   *

They changed trains and ate a quick meal at a place called Grudziaz, an old town on the Vistula. It began to rain as they moved out of Grudziaz and the raindrops pattered against the carriage windows and the land looked sodden and miserable under the weeping skies. Brady still had no idea why they were going to Torun, but no doubt eventually all would be made clear.

He dozed off and awoke suddenly to find that nothing had changed. He looked out of the window and it seemed that the same piece of countryside was rolling past as had been doing so when he closed his eyes.

'How much farther is it?' he asked.

'Not far. About twenty or thirty kilometres. Have you had a good sleep?'

'I've had a lousy sleep,' Brady said. His mouth felt like the inside of an old shoe and his left arm was suffering from an attack of pins and needles. 'Does it always rain?'

'Not always. Sometimes it snows.'

'That's all we need.'

It had stopped raining when they reached Torun. They left the station and got on a bus which rattled away through the same sort of old cobbled streets as they had left behind in Gdansk.

'You've been here before?' Brady asked.

'Yes, I've been here before,' she said; and

72

then added as if by way of a bonus: 'Copernicus was born here, you know.'

'I didn't know,' Brady said; and he tried to remember just what Copernicus had been famous for. Wasn't he the astronomer who first suggested that the earth and the other planets revolved round the sun?

'It was called Thorn when the Germans had it. It was a Prussian frontier town then; now the border is nearly three hundred kilometres farther west.'

'Well, that's how it goes—here today and gone tomorrow.'

He noticed that she frowned slightly, as though the remark had not been to her taste. 'It's easy for you to take it lightly. You English have never known what it is to have a foreigner take your land.'

'That's true,' Brady admitted. 'At least, not lately. There were the Romans, of course, and William the Conqueror, but that was a long time ago. A lot of us are descended from them.'

'For us it is different. Poland is like a nut caught between the two jaws of a giant nutcracker.'

'Russia and Germany?'

'Yes.'

'A pretty tough nut.'

'It hasn't always been tough enough to avoid being crushed.'

That was true, Brady thought; and it could

73

be crushed again. The Poles had to be careful not to step too far out of line. Whatever the people might desire in their hearts, they were well and truly in the Communist bloc and there was not the shadow of a chance of their getting out of it.

The bus rattled along and they passed an open market where there were a lot of horse-drawn carts as well as lorries, stalls, piles of wicker baskets containing vegetables, people milling round.

'This is market day,' Paula said. 'The peasants bring their produce in from the country.'

'So they still have their own farms?'

'A lot of the holdings are privately owned. The fact is they are more productive than the collective farms, so the State tolerates them.'

'The old evil profit motive still works, then?'

'It seems so. Peasants are very reactionary; they simply don't appear to understand the Marxist theory.'

Brady detected a hint of irony. She was not, he would have said, an ardent believer in Marxism herself.

A little later the bus stopped. Paula stood up.

'This is where we get off.'

Brady followed her off the bus and they began to walk. It was quite obvious now that she had been there before; only one who knew the town well could have found the way so

74

unerringly through those crooked, narrow streets and by-ways. What they finally came to was an old three-storey house with tall sash-windows and a steep gabled roof. There were four stone steps leading up to the door, with rusty iron railings on each side, and there was a wrought-iron bell-pull on which Paula gave a tug that produced a harsh grating sound.

'What is this place?' Brady asked.

'It is where we shall stay the night.'

'This is a hotel?'

'No, not a hotel.'

It did not look like one. Nor was there anything to indicate that it might be a boarding-house. It was built of a kind of grey stone, weathered perhaps by centuries of exposure to the elements. The street was quiet, a backwater away from the main current of traffic.

Brady heard the rattle of a bolt; the door was pulled open and a scraggy, elderly woman peered out at them. Paula said something to her in Polish, and whatever the words were, they must have been the right ones, for she opened the door a little wider and stood aside to let them pass.

They found themselves in a dim, tiled hallway from which a spiral flight of stairs led upward. The scraggy woman closed and fastened the door, spoke a couple of words in a singularly rasping voice, and began to climb the stairs.

'Come,' Paula said. She followed the woman.

Brady, carrying his suitcase in his hand, tagged on behind. He was as much in the dark as ever, but soon perhaps some light would penetrate the gloom. And when that happened it might well be enough to blind him.

The room was on the first floor. It was large and the furniture was old and solid. There was a double-bed and there were some chairs and a wardrobe with a mirror on the door, a dressing-table, a window looking out on to the quiet street. The woman showed them in and left them to it; she seemed a taciturn sort, not given to wasting words, and she exhibited not the slightest sign of curiosity regarding the new arrivals. She had obviously been expecting them.

'Does she know you?' Brady asked.

'Well enough.'

'And the house is hers?'

'No, it is not hers.'

He saw that this was another subject on which he was unlikely to receive much information and he asked no further questions.

'You don't object to sharing this room with me?' she asked.

'If you have no objection, why should I?'

'It is necessary, you see.'

'I don't see, but I'm not bothered.'

She gave him a long, searching look as

though trying to read what was in his mind, but he kept his face expressionless and after a few moments she turned away and said: 'We shall go out for a meal. Does that suit you?'

'You're making the arrangements,' Brady said. 'I leave it all to you.'

They waited until evening before going out. There had been nothing to give Brady any uneasiness, but he knew it was too good to last; there would be trouble; there was bound to be, because that was the way of things. There was always trouble—sooner or later.

The restaurant was small and clean and quiet. The food was plain but excellently cooked. Brady, who was feeling really hungry, did full justice to it. Paula observed his hearty appetite with some amusement.

'You like Polish food?'

'It's fine,' Brady said. Now that he had eaten he felt rather less gloomy regarding what fate might have in store for him. The bottle of wine, of which he had drunk the larger share, had helped to put him in better spirits. 'And where do we go from here? The theatre? A film? Opera? You name it.'

She shook her head. 'We are not in Torun for that kind of frivolity. From here we go back to our room.'

Brady shrugged. 'If you say so.' He had been only half serious in suggesting the alternatives; it was rather late to start thinking along those lines anyway.

It was still fine when they left the restaurant. They strolled unhurriedly back to the house in the quiet street, and the scraggy woman let them in. She said nothing, just peered at them with her steely eyes and fastened the door as soon as they were inside. They climbed the stairs to the first floor and the house was as silent as the woman. Paula switched on the light, closed the door of the room and crossed to the window. She drew the curtains; they were on wooden rings which made a clicking noise when they touched, like snooker balls colliding.

Brady looked at his watch. It was just coming up to nine o'clock.

CHAPTER SIX

THE LONG SLEEP

'Smoke if you wish,' she said. 'I don't object.'

Brady was sitting on one of the chairs. Neither he nor the girl had spoken a word for the last ten minutes; they seemed to have run out of conversation.

He shook his head. 'I gave it up. I didn't care for the idea of having bits of lung cut out. Some risks I'm paid to take, but not that.'

'Well, I'm glad,' she said. 'I don't really like cigarette smoke in a room where I'm planning to sleep.'

Brady made no comment.

She sat down at the dressing-table and gazed at her reflection in the glass. She said, without turning her head: 'Eventually we shall have to think about going to bed.'

Brady had in fact been thinking about it for some time, but he did not tell her so.

'After all,' she said, 'there is much to be done tomorrow and it would be ridiculous to sit up all night, don't you think?'

'Very ridiculous.'

'Do you feel tired?'

'A little. Train journeys have that effect on me.'

'If you would like to use the bathroom first,

I don't mind.'

'You can use it first,' Brady said.

'Very well.'

She was away for about twenty minutes. When she came back Brady went to the bathroom. It was at the end of a short passage and about as antique as you could wish. He could hear nobody moving in the house; it was almost eerie in its silence and the sudden gush of water when he turned on a tap was quite startling. He took his time, rather expecting that when he returned to the other room the girl would be in bed. But she was not; she was again sitting at the dressing-table. She was wearing the blue raincoat in place of a dressing-gown; there had obviously been no room in the shoulder-bag for any inessential articles of clothing; and he could see that her feet and legs were bare. He wondered what she had on under the coat—if anything.

She had not turned her head when he came in and she was still not looking at him, unless she could see his reflection as well as her own in the glass. He began to move towards her and came to a halt just behind her chair. Even then she did not turn, but he noticed that she had become very still, scarcely breathing, it seemed. She was certainly aware of his presence behind her. He looked into the glass and saw her eyes watching him. He felt a compulsion to touch her, and he lifted his hand and stroked her cheek lightly with the tips of his fingers.

He was quite unprepared for the effect of this simple act. It was as though the contact of his fingers had given her a galvanic shock, bringing her into sudden life. She turned and rose from the chair in one quick, sinuous movement; and then her arms were round his neck and her mouth was on his; and he was not sure whether it was just the impulse of the moment or whether she had planned it that way. He was not much worried, either; he was happy to go along with anything she had in mind; and his own arms were round her now and the blood was beginning to sing in his veins, or his arteries, or wherever it was that blood did sing. If it sang. And who gave a damn whether it sang or not? For it was surely the old magic getting to work in him—and maybe in her too; the old, old magic that had moved King David when he saw Bath-sheba at her toilet and Romeo when he kissed Juliet at the Capulets' ball; magic old as life itself and new as the dawn light in the eastern sky.

After a while she drew away from him. Her breathing was rapid and he could see that the raincoat was not buttoned; it was just fastened loosely with the belt. It had pulled open and he saw that she was in fact wearing a nightdress under it; but it was a pretty diaphanous nightdress at that and not hiding much of her; and what he couldn't see he could guess at, and it made the blood do a bit more of the

81

singing act.

'You know this is not what we are supposed to do,' she said.

'My instructions were vague enough to embrace almost anything.'

She gave a bewitching smile. 'Even a nice young Polish girl?'

'Especially a nice young Polish girl,' Brady said.

'But you must not forget what we have to do tomorrow.'

'I don't even know what we have to do tomorrow.'

'So don't you think we had better go to bed and then perhaps I will tell you.'

'That sounds like the best idea I've heard in quite some time,' Brady said.

*   *   *

He ran his fingers through the blonde hair, invisible in the darkness but beautifully soft to the touch. 'I don't understand,' he said. 'I just don't understand.'

'What don't you understand, Walter?'

That name again! It still irked him. He would have liked to tell her to call him Steve, but it might not have been wise.

'Why you do this.'

'Why I do what? Let you make love to me? Is that what you mean?'

'No, not that. Why you do this intelligence

82

work for a foreign power. Do you hate your country?'

She made a sudden movement away from him. 'How can you say that? I love Poland. I would die for my country.'

'But you are working against Poland.'

'No; I am working against the Communist Government. That is what I hate.'

'Why do you hate the Communists?'

'Because they are traitors. They are the tools of Soviet Russia.'

'And you hate Russia?'

'Of course.'

'Why?'

'Do you need to ask that?' she said. 'Have you never heard of Katyn?'

'Katyn! Isn't that where some Polish soldiers were killed?'

'Some Polish soldiers!' Anger had hardened her voice. 'Fourteen thousand officers. The élite of our army. And they were not just killed; they were murdered, shot in the back of the head while their hands were tied behind them; then thrown into a mass grave. Fourteen thousand of them. Massacred by the Russians.'

'But can you be sure of that? Didn't the Russians maintain that the Germans did it?'

'Of course. And they tried to make it seem so, but they were clumsy even in that, and nobody has any doubt that it was they who really did it.'

'Still,' Brady said, 'it was a long time ago.

You weren't even born.'

'Does it matter how long ago it was? It was a terrible crime against our nation. Two of my uncles were killed at Katyn.'

Brady could see why she was so vehement; she had reason to be. And that business at Katyn was not the only crime which the Russians had committed against the Poles; there were plenty of others, going back a long way, back into the recesses of history. No more than the Germans had committed perhaps; hadn't they murdered six million Poles in World War Two? But that was another matter.

'So now do you understand?'

'Yes,' Brady said, 'I understand now.'

'I begin to wish,' she said later, giving a faint sigh, 'that tomorrow might never come.'

'Why?' Brady asked.

'Because tomorrow I must hand you over.'

He felt his heart give a jolt. After all she had said about hating the Communists, was she now going to confess that she was nevertheless working for them? Was she going to tell him that she had been deceiving him and that tomorrow she was going to turn him in? Suddenly the old magic seemed to have turned a little sour.

'Hand me over?'

'To the man who is going to take you on from here. He will be coming in the morning. Then I don't see you any more.'

He began to breathe more easily; his brief

suspicion had been unfounded; it was not the Secret Police to whom she was to hand him over but merely another agent. Yet he failed to see the necessity.

'Why? Why can't you go along with me? Why does this damned man have to take over?'

'Because that's the way it has been arranged.'

'Well, I don't like the arrangement. I'm perfectly happy with you.'

She snuggled closer to him. 'And I am happy with you. But we don't have any choice. We have to do it the way it's planned.'

'So from tomorrow you fade out of the picture?'

'Yes.'

'I think that's one hell of a bad plan.'

'There's nothing we can do about it.' She sounded sad. She was not liking it much, either.

But she was right; there was nothing they could do about it. They were just puppets and somebody else was pulling the strings; they didn't even know for what purpose the strings were being pulled.

'Well,' he said, 'if that's the way it is, if tomorrow is to be goodbye, we may as well make the most of what time we have left.'

She made no objection to that. There might have been nothing about it in the plan, but she made no objection.

'What time is he supposed to come?' Brady asked.

'At ten o'clock.'

Brady looked at his watch. 'It's a quarter to ten now. Do you think he'll be punctual?'

'Yes, he'll be punctual.'

They had breakfasted at a small and rather grubby café which seemed to be patronised largely by working men. Brady had been in low spirits; he knew he was going to miss Paula and he was prepared to hate the man who was taking over from her on sight. Maybe this time it really would be a furtive little character in a shabby raincoat. Paula seemed scarcely more cheerful than he felt, so maybe she was going to miss him, too; maybe there had been more to their relationship than a brief one-night passion; maybe, given the chance, something more permanent could have grown from it. But the chance was not going to be given; when the man came that would be it, the finish, the end of the affair. Goodbye and thanks; it was lovely while it lasted.

He glanced at his watch again. 'It's gone ten. I don't see anybody. Maybe he forgot the appointment.'

'He wouldn't forget.'

'Well, maybe he changed his mind.'

'He wouldn't do that, either.'

'Do you know him?'

'Yes, I know him.'

'What's his name?'

'Henryk Szydiak.'

Brady walked to the window and looked down into the street. Two girls rode past on bicycles; a man was pushing a handcart over the cobbles; a woman on the opposite pavement was carrying what looked like a bundle of washing under her arm. There was no sign of anyone who might have been Henryk Szydiak.

'I think it might be best not to stand there,' Paula suggested.

Brady moved away from the window. 'You think someone could be watching the house?'

'I don't think it's likely, but there is no point in taking unnecessary risks.'

Another hour passed. They were not talking much. Brady guessed that they were both thinking of the one subject—Henryk Szydiak; both wondering what in hell could have happened to him.

'Do you still believe he's coming?'

'He must come,' Paula said; but she sounded uneasy. Perhaps she was wondering what to do if Szydiak did not come.

'Maybe he overslept.'

She answered nothing to that. He could tell she was on edge. She would sit down on a chair, but after a minute or two she would get up again; she would go to the dressing-table and start combing her hair, which was in no need of such attention, but soon she would drop the comb and once again move restlessly about the room. She went to the window, though she had told him it was not wise to do so.

Finally, at twelve o'clock, she said abruptly: 'I must go and look for him. Something must have happened.'

'Where will you look? Have you any idea where he might be?'

'I know where he lodges. I will go there.'

Brady was not sure it was at all a good idea. 'Wouldn't that be taking a big risk? If anything has happened, going to his place might be to walk into a trap.'

'There is that risk,' she admitted, 'but it will have to be taken.'

'I don't agree.'

'Can you think of any better idea?'

'We could go back to Gdansk.'

'That would get us nowhere.'

'It would get us out of here, which I'm beginning to think would not be at all a bad thing. Our friend Henryk should have been here at ten; it's now twelve and he still isn't here; that means something has gone wrong with the plan. Well, to my way of thinking when a plan starts to go wrong that's the time to get out, before the roof falls in.'

'We can't just walk away and forget it.'

'I can.'

'No,' she said; and she sounded very firm

about it; 'I can't do that and I can't let you do it. I will go and look for Henryk.'

She was already putting on her raincoat and he saw that she was determined to go, whatever he might say. He gave a sigh of resignation; some people were so damned conscientious.

'All right then, if you're set on it. But I'm coming with you.'

She shook her head. 'No; it is better if I go alone.'

'It is not better if you go alone. Do you think I'm going to stick around here wondering what the devil's going on?' He had a vision of himself waiting in the room for her to come back and having the door kicked open by a couple of goons from the Secret Police instead. If there was going to be trouble he preferred to go and meet it rather than wait for it to catch up with him. The best way of all, of course, would have been to follow his first suggestion and leg it out of there in double quick time, but Paula seemed to have a rooted objection to that, so he would just have to go along with her. But one thing he was not going to do was stay in that room while she went hunting around for Henryk Szydiak.

She looked at him. 'Are you afraid I might not come back?'

'The thought did cross my mind.'

'Very well, if it pleases you, I suppose you had better come.'

89

'It doesn't please me,' Brady said. 'It just displeases me marginally less than staying here on my Tod.'

*   *   *

It was quite a way, but they walked. There was a cramped little grocery shop on the ground floor and there was a bald-headed, sad-looking man slicing bacon for a customer as though he didn't much care if he carved his own fingers off in the process. There was also a stout woman who could have been the bald man's wife packing some bags of sugar on a shelf. Paula spoke to the woman while Brady stood and waited, unable to understand a word. There was only the one customer, an elderly woman in a black dress; she looked harmless, Brady thought. He was ready to suspect everyone he saw of being a security agent or a secret policeman, but he was prepared to eliminate the woman in the black dress from suspicion—just.

Paula finished talking to the stout woman, and the woman walked to a door at the back of the shop and Paula followed. Brady tagged on as well; he wanted to keep close to the girl. There was a kind of lobby behind the shop and a flight of stairs. The stout woman halted at the foot of the stairs, pointed upward and said something more to Paula, who nodded as if to indicate that she understood and began to ascend. Brady squeezed past the stout woman and caught up with the girl half-way up the stairs.

'What did she say?'

'She said the room is the second one on the right.'

'Did she say if Szydiak was in?'

'She said she hadn't seen him since last night when he came in very drunk.'

'Drunk!'

They had reached the landing. Paula stopped and turned to him. The stout woman had gone back to the shop.

'She said she saw him come in and he was staggering. She thought he was going to fall, but he didn't. She was surprised he managed to get up the stairs.'

'Did she say anything to him?'

'Yes, but he didn't answer. He just went up the stairs and into his room. She hasn't seen him go out today, so she imagines he's sleeping it off.'

'It sounds likely,' Brady said. He remembered reading somewhere that in one respect the Poles were very much like the Americans and Russians—and the French, too, if it came to that: they had a drink problem. So he had been given a guide who hit the bottle. That was fine; that was really fine and dandy; it was all he wanted. 'Well, we'd better go and see.'

Paula tapped on the door with her knuckles.

91

There was no response, no sound of any movement inside the room. She turned the knob and pushed. The door was not locked; it opened with a faint squeak of unoiled hinges. They went into the room.

The man was not in the bed; he was lying on it. He had not bothered to undress and he even had his shoes on; there was a lot of mud on them and some of it had transferred itself to the bed-cover. He was lying on his back and his hair was a tangled thicket. He was a craggy, broad-shouldered man, but the skin of his face had a greyish tinge. There was a dark shadow of stubble on his chin and cheeks.

'Henryk!' the girl said. 'Henryk!'

He did not wake. They moved in closer and looked down at him. He was sleeping sure enough, even though his eyes were open and staring; but it was the long sleep and he was never going to wake. Henryk Szydiak had drunk his last vodka.

CHAPTER SEVEN

NEW ORDERS

But it was not vodka that had killed him; it was probably not even vodka that had made him unsteady on his feet when the woman had seen him come in the previous evening. And if she had looked at him a little more closely she might have seen the blood. But perhaps the light had been poor and perhaps her eyesight was not as good as it had once been. Or maybe she had simply not been interested.

He had dripped plenty of blood on to the bed; there was a big dark stain where it had leaked out of him. His right arm was crossed over his chest and the hand was inside the jacket just above the waist. It was probably where the wound was; he might still have been trying to staunch the flow of blood when he died. It was a wonder he had got so far; the stairs must have been a hell of a climb for a man in his condition. It was a wonder, too, that he had not dripped blood on the stairs. But maybe he had at that, a few drops; the light was none too good out there even in daytime and no one would be looking for blood.

'So this is Henryk.'

'Yes.' The girl's voice was low, shocked.

'He's no use to us now.'

So much was obvious. A dead man was not going to guide anyone anywhere—except maybe the way he had gone.

'What did he do?'

'Do?' She seemed not to understand the question.

'What was his job? The kind of work he was going to do for us wasn't a full-time occupation, was it?'

'I don't suppose so.'

'But you don't know what his legitimate trade was?'

'No. I didn't know him so well.'

Brady dropped the subject; it was of no importance; it had just been something to say. What was important was that Szydiak had been in a fight. Somebody had tried to kill him. Correction—somebody had killed him. But he had got away; he had reached base in spite of being hit, so presumably he had dished out some of the same treatment.

'Did he carry a gun?'

'I don't know. Possibly.'

And possibly it was still on him. Brady felt no irresistible urge to find out by searching him. Neither of them touched Szydiak; neither of them wanted to; there was no need to feel his pulse to be sure he was dead.

But if Szydiak had been in a fight there could be only one likely reason for that: the opposition had been on his tail and had moved in on him. And that was not good at all, because if they had been on Szydiak's tail it might not be so long before they got on to his. He was beginning to feel pretty sick, and the sight of Szydiak's dead face and Szydiak's blood staining the bed-cover did nothing to improve matters. He turned to the girl; the colour was coming back into her cheeks and she seemed to be recovering remarkably quickly from the shock of finding a corpse where she had been expecting a live man.

'It looks to me,' Brady said, 'as if he had the hounds snapping at his heels. Does it look that way to you?'

'Yes,' she said, 'it does.'

'So don't you think it's time we were getting out of here?' He was listening for the sound of heavy feet on the stairs. They were like sitting ducks in that room. He was relieved to find that she was inclined to agree with him again.

'Yes,' she said, 'I do think so.'

There were more customers in the shop when they went down, and the sad-looking man and the stout woman were both busy. Paula spoke a few words to the woman and she nodded as though in agreement, and then they were out of the shop. They turned left and walked away.

Brady was half expecting somebody to come up and arrest them, but nobody did; so maybe Szydiak had killed the tail before coming home to die.

'What did you say to the woman?' he asked.

'I told her that Henryk was still not feeling very well and it would be best if she let him sleep on without being disturbed. With luck it may be quite some time before they find he is dead.'

'The longer, the better. Anyway, one thing is certain now—this is really the end of the line. Now I pack my traps and go home.'

'You can't do that,' she said quickly.

'Can't I! Just watch and you'll see I can.'

They were walking at a brisk pace, but not so fast as to make themselves conspicuous; it would have been foolish to give the impression that they were running away from something.

She said, a trifle acidly: 'I can't think why they sent a man like you on this assignment. You don't seem to have your heart in it.'

'Is that how it appears to you?'

'Yes, it is.'

'Well, you're right; I haven't got my heart in it, and I never had. And if you'd really like to know, I'll tell you why they sent me—because I'm not a real cut-and-dried professional; I'm just somebody they keep on ice for jobs like this. A real professional would want to know what in hell was going on, you see; he'd want to know why he was doing this or that and they'd have to put him in the picture. But me, they don't have to tell a thing, not a damned thing. I can be left in the dark. I can be sent on a blind date.'

The expression was apparently new to her.

'Blind date?'

'That's what they call it when somebody arranges an evening out for you with a girl you've never seen.'

'So I'm your blind date?'

'You're part of it. The best part. But here's another thing—how much do you know about what's going on?'

'How do you mean?'

'Well, for instance, do you know why I'm here?'

'No,' she admitted, 'I don't know that.'

'I thought not. All you know is that you had to make contact with me and bring me to Torun and hand me over to Henryk Szydiak. Right?'

She had to confess that it was so. 'But there is no reason why I should be told more. It is safer if I do not know.'

'So that if anyone interrogates you, you can't tell them anything important? Even if they tear your nails out you can't squeak.'

'Of course.'

'We're two of a kind, aren't we?' Brady said. 'Know nothing, tell nothing. Bloody pawns. Expendable. Only I don't happen to care for the idea of being expended, so that's why I'm pulling out.'

'And what do you think your people in London will say about that?'

'I don't care what they say,' Brady said. But he did. In their view the death of Szydiak might not be considered sufficient reason for a precipitate withdrawal. Yet how could he go any further now that he had no guide, even if he wanted to?

'Perhaps you shouldn't make any hasty decision,' Paula said. 'At least not until I have received new orders.'

'New orders! How are you going to get them?'

'In an emergency such as this I have a telephone number to ring.'

Brady was amazed. 'You're proposing to use the telephone? You must be crazy. Suppose the line is tapped.'

'It quite possibly may be. But don't worry; it will be all right; the conversation will appear completely innocent; there are ways of saying things so that no outsider can understand.'

Brady was not entirely reassured; it still seemed to be taking a great risk. But once again he was overruled by the girl's determination.

'We will go in here,' she said.

It was a café. There were some tables and chairs, a small counter on one side. It was fairly crowded at that hour, but they found seats at one of the tables and Paula ordered coffee and sandwiches. Brady had never felt less like eating; Henryk Szydiak lying dead in his own blood had pretty effectively killed his appetite. But Paula told him he must eat something if only for the look of the thing, and it might be advisable anyway, since there was no telling when they would have their next meal. Brady did his best, but he was ill at ease; there was a long-nosed man at a nearby table who was showing rather too much interest in the girl. There might, of course, be nothing sinister in that, seeing that she was the kind of girl any man could well be interested in, but he did not like it nevertheless. When she got up to make the telephone call the long-nosed man followed her with his eyes.

The telephone was in a kind of alcove near the counter. Brady could see Paula speaking into it, and the conversation seemed to be taking quite a time; which was bad, because if anyone was trying to trace the origin of the call they would probably be able to do so without difficulty. But at last she hung the receiver up and came back to the table. And maybe it had not been so very long really; maybe it had just seemed long to him.

'What did they say?' he asked.

'They said I would have to do Henryk's job.'

'You mean you're to take me on from here?'

'Yes.'

He was not sure whether he felt pleased or not. Certainly he was glad she was going to stay with him; but it meant that things were still going ahead more or less as planned; the death of Szydiak had not knocked it all on the head. Perhaps it had been too much to hope that it might; evidently there were people who attached far more importance to the operation than he did.

'But do you know where to go?'

'They told me—naturally.'

Naturally, they would.

Brady started chewing on a piece of sandwich which seemed to have been made from a slice of dried horsemeat, and then he heard a rather deep voice make some remark, presumably in Polish. He glanced up and saw that the long-nosed man had decided to do more than simply look at Paula; he had walked over to the table and was speaking to her.

Brady's heart skipped a beat and he almost choked on the sandwich. The long-nosed man had a sallow complexion and heavy shoulders; he was wearing a dark suit, not very well cut, and there was a bulge under the left arm which could well have been made by a gun in a holster. He said a few words to Paula and then glanced at Brady with a pair of eyes that were about as cold and unfriendly as a cobra's. Brady felt like jumping up and making a run for it before the gun came out, but that would have been a crazy thing to do, so he sat where he was and gazed straight back at the long-nosed man, doing his best to appear innocent while feeling as guilty as a safe-breaker caught in the act of setting off the gelignite. Fortunately there was no need to keep it up for long, because Paula said something and the long-nosed man's eyes swung back to her so promptly Brady almost expected to hear them click. After that he said a few more words, gave a slight bow, turned and walked away.

The sweat had collected under Brady's armpits and it felt cold and clammy. He managed to get the piece of half-chewed sandwich down his gullet and he looked at the girl and said: 'What did he want?'

'He wanted to tell me that he recognised me.'

'Recognised you!'

'From the Zoppotski. He has been in Gdansk and seen my act. He admires me very much; he wanted me to know that.'

'I thought he was a policeman.'

She smiled. 'Did he scare you?'

'You bet he scared me. What's more, I don't think he likes me very much.'

'He likes me.'

'That could be the reason.'

'Finish your sandwich,' she said; 'then we'll go.'

'We'll go without finishing it. I've eaten as much as I can take of that.'

They left the café and started walking back to the house where they had spent the night.

'Are we leaving at once?' Brady asked.

'It would be best.'

He got the impression that she felt it might not be altogether safe to stay any longer at the house. The death of Henryk Szydiak could hardly have been called reassuring, to say the least; and the sooner they were out of Torun the better it might be. Not that anywhere else was likely to be very safe either, but somewhere a bit further away from the dead man would certainly be preferable.

'And where do we go from here?'

'To Leszno.'

'Where's that?'

'About fifty kilometres the other side of Poznan.'

'You're taking me on quite a tour of the country, aren't you?'

'It was not my idea.' She sounded just a trifle snappish; possibly she was feeling the nervous strain, too; it would have been surprising if it had been otherwise.

When they were approaching the street where the house was she came to a stop and said: 'I think it might be advisable for you to wait here. I will get the luggage.'

'Why?'

'Because it would be better that way.'

'You think they could be watching the house, don't you?'

'I don't think it's likely, but it is possible. There is no point in both of us taking the risk.'

Brady was not whole-heartedly in favour of the proposal. There might be reason in it, but he had an unreasoning reluctance to be separated from his guide.

'How can you carry everything?'

'One suitcase and a shoulder-bag! Do you

take me for an invalid?'

'I'd rather come with you, all the same.'

'Now please don't be awkward,' she said. 'This is no time to argue. Stay here, Walter. I will not be long, I promise you.'

Brady gave in. She could be very persuasive.

'All right then; but for God's sake be careful.'

'What else would I be?' she said.

He watched her until she turned the corner and was out of sight. He was sorry to see her go and was uneasy for her sake; she might be as careful as could be and yet be caught. It was a possibility he hated to contemplate, but it was one he found himself unable to get out of his mind. Suppose they were waiting in the room; suppose they grabbed her as soon as she opened the door. The more he thought about it, the more likely it seemed. He should never have let her go; they should have abandoned the luggage and got away from there while they had the chance. Why take such a risk for the sake of a few articles of clothing? Why had he ever let her go?

There was a small square where he was waiting, some flower-beds and one or two trees not yet in leaf. The houses round the square were all old and weathered, like so many in Torun, and a few of them had iron balconies outside the first floor windows. He saw a woman looking towards him from one of these balconies, and he shifted his position because he felt he must be making himself conspicuous by standing there. When he glanced again at the balcony the woman had gone. He could imagine her going to the telephone and reporting to the police a suspicious-looking person loitering in the square, but then he told himself it was nonsense; getting the jitters was not going to help either himself or Paula.

He was jittery, nevertheless. He walked to the corner where he had lost sight of her and peered cautiously round it. He recognised the street where the house was and he thought he could see it in the distance with its four stone steps and iron railings, but he could not be absolutely certain it was the one. He could see no one watching it, but there was no sign of the girl, either. She should have been on the way back by this time. How long did it take to collect a suitcase and a shoulder-bag from the first floor? But maybe she was talking to the scraggy woman. And maybe she was never coming back. There was a car parked not far from the house and he was not sure he cared much for that, either.

One thing was certain—he had better not hang around there, peering furtively round the corner; that was one sure way of making himself really conspicuous. He moved away and was soon back at the square. His mind was going like an old gramophone record with the needle stuck in a groove, churning out the same scrap of tune over and over again. Suppose she never came back! What did he do then? Get the hell out of there? That would be a pretty spineless thing to do; to run away and leave her to work out her own salvation. Yet it was what she had obviously intended he should do if the situation arose, even if she had not actually said as much. And what help would it be to her if he went to the house looking for her? It would simply mean that he would be nabbed as well. What the devil was he to do?

Time was certainly slipping away now. He walked to the corner again and still there was no sign of her. It couldn't have taken her as long as this, not if things had gone smoothly. Something must have gone wrong. And then he noticed that the parked car was no longer there, and he was not happy about that, not happy at all.

He hesitated for about ten more seconds and then decided he had had enough of it; he couldn't take any more of the uncertainty; he just had to find out what had happened to her, whatever the consequences. He turned the corner and began to walk towards the house.

He had covered about half the distance when he saw her come out lugging his suitcase in her right hand and with the bag slung over her left shoulder. He caught a glimpse of the scraggy woman shutting the door, and then Paula had taken the four steps to the pavement and was walking towards him.

She was angry with him; he could see that at once.

'You were supposed to stay where I left you. Why are you here? Why didn't you wait?'

Brady took his suitcase from her hand and they walked on side by side. 'I was worried about you.'

'Worried!'

'You were taking so long. I thought something might have happened.'

'To me?'

'Yes, to you.'

'And supposing something had happened to me, what did you intend to do?'

'I don't know.'

'Were you proposing to come charging to the rescue like a knight in shining armour?'

Her sarcasm nettled him. He said with a touch of asperity: 'Well, I can see that anything in that line wouldn't have been appreciated. So maybe I should have walked the other way.'

'Oh, Walter,' she said, and her voice had softened, 'you are such a fool. Where was the point of me going to the house alone if you were coming to look for me as soon as you thought I had been gone too long?'

'I don't know. But did you imagine I would clear out and leave you, just like that?'

'That is what you were supposed to do.'

'All right, so I didn't do what I was supposed to do. What kept you so long?'

'A man came to the door when I was

upstairs. I thought it best to wait until he had gone.'

'A man. What did he want?'

'He told the woman he was from one of the ministries, checking on the number of people occupying each house.'

'Do you think that was the truth?'

'It could have been.'

'But you think it might not.'

'Who can say? Thieves sometimes pose as officials to get into houses.'

'It's not thieves we have to worry about,' Brady said. 'Do you think he could still be hanging around?'

'No; he went away in a car.'

Brady remembered the car he had seen. 'That hardly looks as though he was going to every house.'

'No.'

'You think he could have been from the Secret Police?'

'I don't know,' she said. 'And it's no use speculating on who he might have been. What we have to do now is find out the time of the next train leaving for Leszno.'

There seemed to be no sense in arguing about that.

CHAPTER EIGHT

PARTY

They had to wait nearly an hour for the train and Brady was on edge the whole time. Paula looked outwardly calm, but he felt pretty certain she was edgy too. There was no certainty, of course, that anyone was on to them; the fact that Szydiak had been killed proved nothing. In fact the killing might have had nothing whatever to do with Szydiak's undercover work; he might have received his injury in a brawl or might have been waylaid by a thug out to commit a robbery; there were a hundred ways he could have got a hole in him big enough to let his life seep away drop by drop.

But Brady was not convincing himself by thinking along those lines. He knew why Szydiak had died, and the only question was whether friend Henryk had choked off the pursuit by killing his assailant. And if so, how much information had the other man passed back to his bosses before he handed in his chips? In the circumstances an hour's wait for a train was very trying indeed.

But the train came at last and a little later they were dragging out of Torun on the first leg of the journey to Leszno, where he presumed he would meet someone else who might or might not know why he had been sent there and what the devil it was all about. It was all very tiring, very confusing, very wearing to the nerves, and had only one bright spot as far as he could see: a girl named Paula Nowicki.

'You do not look happy, Walter,' she said.

'Should I be?' Brady asked.

'There are reasons. Things could be worse.'

'Tell me how.'

'It is obvious that nobody knows about us.'

'How do you figure that?'

'If they had known, we should have been arrested at the station. Since we were not picked up there I think we can safely assume that we may now relax a little.'

She was cool, Brady thought. It was apparent from what she had just said that she had been half expecting trouble at the station at Torun. But she had accepted the risk, and as nothing had happened she was feeling fine; she was not allowing any apprehensions concerning what might lie ahead to disturb her. Brady wished he could have taken things as easily; the prospect disturbed him plenty.

They had to wait half an hour for the connection at Poznan. There were crowds of people milling around and the customary uniformed policemen keeping an eye on things. Any kind of uniform tended to have a bad effect on Brady's nervous system, and he was not at all sorry to be packed into another train and to leave Poznan behind. Even the fact, communicated to him by his attractive guide, who seemed to be a veritable mine of information when she put her mind to it, that this was the birthplace of Field Marshal von Hindenburg, having at that time been a German city named Posen, failed to give him any particular joy. He did momentarily try to imagine Hindenburg as a baby yelling his head off in a Posen cradle, but the mind shuddered a bit and passed on to more pressing matters, such as how in hell he was to get out of this benighted country and back to dear old London, where all you had to worry about were simple little things like a couple of hard boys knocking the stuffing out of you to oblige a friend. Happy days.

It was getting on into the evening when the train drew in at Leszno, and it was already growing dark. Brady reflected gloomily that there are few things in life more depressing than to arrive in darkness in a strange town where you don't know a soul and where you have never had the slightest desire to be.

But Paula, strangely enough, seemed remarkably cheerful. Maybe she was thinking that she would soon be shot of him, and then she could go back to Gdansk and singing at the Zoppotski. Maybe.

It was not such a large station as the one at Poznan, but it was a junction and there were plenty of people lugging suitcases and doing all

110

the other things people did on railway stations.

'Have you been here before?' Brady asked.

'No,' she said, 'never.'

'Will there be someone to meet us?'

'That is unlikely.'

'So what do we do now?'

'We get a taxi of course. I have the address.'

He should have thought of that for himself, but after the long train journey his brain seemed to be working a trifle sluggishly.

'Don't worry,' she said. 'Everything is under control.'

Perhaps it was, he thought, for the present. But the question was, how long would everything remain under control? How long before the gears stripped, the steering-wheel came off, the brake linings wore out and the whole crazy machine went careering downhill at a hundred miles to the hour? Would somebody tell him that?

There seemed to be a brisk demand for taxis, and they had to wait in a queue for nearly half an hour before getting one. It was a chilly, cheerless evening and Brady had no difficulty in feeling chilly and cheerless also. He was thankful when they reached the head of the queue and got a taxi at last. Paula told the driver the address and they got in.

It turned out to be quite a way, well out on the western fringes of the town in a quiet sideroad which was very poorly lighted. The driver of the taxi seemed glad to be rid of them, and as soon as he had been paid he drove quickly away, as though afraid they might change their minds and ask him to take them somewhere else instead. The place looked uninviting enough to give anyone second thoughts. There was a wooden fence and an iron gate standing open, and beyond the gate a kind of drive led away past the dark shapes of trees and what appeared to be a neglected and overgrown garden. No house was visible, but there obviously had to be one, so they set off up the drive and sure enough a building very soon loomed up ahead. There were a few gleams of light coming from it, indicating perhaps that the windows were shuttered or heavily curtained, and they managed to find their way to the front door which was tucked away under a porch.

'I don't think anybody's expecting us,' Brady said.

'Did you think they'd be waiting on the doorstep?' Paula asked. 'Why don't you ring the bell?'

Brady dumped his suitcase and searched for the bell, but without success. 'There doesn't seem to be one.'

There was, however, an iron knocker. The girl stepped forward and did some vigorous work on it, making such a clatter that Brady's nerves started protesting again; it sounded loud enough to attract attention for miles around. But it had the desired effect; the door was opened almost immediately and a man looked out. The light was at his back and it was difficult to get a clear impression of his face, but he must have had a better view of them and it was obvious that he realised who they were. He said something in Polish and Paula answered. Then she turned to Brady.

'You were wrong. We are expected.'

She walked into the house and Brady picked up his suitcase and followed. The man closed the door and bolted it. They could see him more clearly now; he appeared to be about sixty and his hair was greying, he had something of the look of a soldier, holding himself very stiffly, shoulders set well back. He spoke again in Polish and again Paula answered. Then he turned to Brady and said: 'You are English, so we speak English. My name is Relke. Welcome to my house.'

He held out his hand and Brady shook it. It felt hard and bony and very dry; Relke himself gave an impression of being hard and dry and bony.

'You have heard what happened in Torun?' Paula asked. 'Why I have had to come on here.'

'I hear that Henryk is killed,' Relke said. 'That is bad. But you have no trouble?'

'No.'

'Good. You know what happens now?'

'My part is finished. I go back to Gdansk.'

'Do you have to do that?' Brady asked.

113

'Can't you stick around a bit longer?'

'It would not be as planned.'

'I don't care how it's planned; I like having you with me. I have a feeling you bring me luck.'

'Is that the only reason you wish to keep me with you? Because I bring you luck.'

'There are other reasons,' Brady said.

Relke was looking at them and smiling a little; he seemed to have very quickly sized up the situation, to have a shrewd suspicion of what the other reasons might be.

He said to the girl: 'Why talk of hurrying away so quickly? No sense to go tonight anyway. Tonight we have a party. You should join. You can sleep here. Tomorrow we see.'

From the moment of entering the house Brady had been aware of a considerable amount of noise in the background, and when Relke mentioned the word 'party' he knew what it was: a lot of people all talking together, now and then a burst of laughter.

'Come,' Relke said. 'Give me your coats. Later I show you where to sleep. Now we go to party. Your man is there.'

It was a large room, brilliantly lighted. It was crowded with people, men and women, everyone drinking, talking, laughing, gesticulating excitedly. Brady wondered what they were celebrating—if anything. There were chairs and sofas, and some of the guests were sitting down, but most of them seemed to prefer to stand. A few looked round when Relke ushered the two newcomers into the room, but the majority were too engrossed in their own conversation to take any notice. Relke beckoned to a young man who was with a group on the left and the man came over to them.

Relke introduced him. 'This is Jan Zalski. He is to take you where you have to go, Mr Storey.'

Zalski grinned and shook hands. His hand was as hard and bony as Relke's, but the grip was stronger. Zalski himself looked strong and solid; he had long dark hair and a pale, narrow face, and he was wearing a check shirt, open at the throat, and a pair of black trousers supported by a wide leather belt with a brass buckle.

'Glad to see you, Mr Storey. There is complication, I hear.'

'You could call it that,' Brady said.

Zalski turned to Paula. 'So you must bring him here instead.'

'Yes.'

With his black, unkempt hair and brilliant dark eyes, Zalski had, Brady thought, a curiously wild look about him. Too wild perhaps.

'Okay,' Zalski said. 'You hungry? Plenty food. Help yourselves.'

There was a big sideboard looking like an offshoot from a delicatessen store—all kinds of sausages, pressed meats, salads, pickles, soused herrings, cheeses, loaves of bread.

'Later,' Paula said.

Relke, having made the introduction, had drifted away.

Zalski said: 'I get you vodka.' He went to the sideboard and poured three glasses of the spirit from a bottle, one for each of them.

It was strong vodka. When Brady took a taste of it, it seemed to blaze a trail of fire all the way down to his stomach. Zalski grinned at him.

'Good?'

'Strong.'

'Drink like this,' Zalski said. He emptied his own glass down his throat without appearing to swallow.

A young, starved-looking man stood on a chair and began to recite. It could have been verse; it had rhythm and sounded exciting. The others stopped talking to listen; at the end they gave the young man an ovation. They drank to him with enthusiasm.

Zalski said: 'Is poem about Poland. Heroes, warriors, battles, all that.'

There was a piano. A man sat down and played some Chopin pieces, waltz, mazurka, polonaise. Brady could see tears in many eyes; the emotional effect was being felt all round. Then they began to sing. Some girls started dancing in the middle of the room; men joined in; it became wilder; the noise increased; the bottles of vodka were emptied one by one and Relke went for more. Zalski had moved away.

Brady and Paula went to the sideboard and helped themselves to food.

'I'm not sure we ought to be here,' Brady said.

She seemed surprised. 'But this is the place I had to bring you to. There has been no mistake.'

'I know that. I meant this party. It looks like turning into a rowdy evening. They all mean to get drunk. A lot of them are already.'

'It doesn't matter.'

'I should have preferred something a little quieter.'

'You are worrying again, Walter.'

'It's the way I'm made.'

'Drink some more vodka; it will make you feel better.'

'I'll tell you a secret,' Brady said. 'I hate vodka.'

She gave a laugh. 'You'd better not mention that too loudly in here. Some of them speak English.'

One of the English-speaking men introduced himself to Brady a while later. He looked about fifty and had grey hair, short and stiff like a fibre doormat. His eyes were so pale as to be almost colourless and he was wearing steel-rimmed glasses. His complexion would have made a ball of putty seem flushed and his nose was nipped in at the nostrils, as though someone had put a clip on it when it had been young and malleable.

'My name is Edward Malkowicz.' He stared hard at Brady and appeared to be perfectly sober. 'I believe you have just come from England, Mr Storey.'

Brady supposed Zalski had been talking, or Relke perhaps. There seemed to be no point in denying the fact. 'I have.'

'And you are here on business, perhaps?'

'No, not business.'

'You are on holiday?'

'Yes.'

'Do you know,' Malkowicz said, 'it would never have occurred to me that anyone would come from London to Leszno for a holiday. It seems so improbable.'

'What makes you suppose I come from London?'

Malkowicz made a fluttering gesture with his hand. 'Ah, forgive me. One is so apt to think that all Englishmen come from London. It is not so, of course.'

'Of course. And I am not staying in Leszno.'

'Ah, so you are travelling on?'

'Well, yes,' Brady said, and wondered how the devil he had allowed the conversation to take this line. He did not care for Malkowicz and he did not care for the questions the man asked; he seemed to be altogether too inquisitive. He spoke very correct English, but with an accent; there were a lot of Polish immigrants in Britain who spoke like that.

'With the charming Miss Nowicki?'

'It's possible.'

'You are here on a mission, perhaps?' Malkowicz suggested, with sly insinuation.

Brady was startled. 'A mission!'

'A secret mission. One about which you must not talk.'

Brady gave a laugh, which sounded, he thought, about as phoney as a street salesman's patter. 'What do you take me for? A spy?'

'Why, of course, Mr Storey,' Malkowicz said. 'What else?' And he laughed too.

Brady joined in the laughter, as though appreciating the joke; but he was not at all sure that Malkowicz was joking, that was the devil of it; he was not sure about that at all.

Having made his joke or his point or whatever it was, Malkowicz soon moved away. Brady looked for Paula and saw her talking to Zalski. He joined them and broke into the conversation without ceremony.

'I've just been accused of being a spy.'

Zalski seemed unmoved by the statement, but Paula said quickly: 'Who said that?'

'A man named Edward Malkowicz. He cornered me and started asking questions. Very pointed questions.'

Zalski slapped him on the shoulder. 'Ah, that is so like Edward. He likes to be playing such games. He is working in a bank. Is dull life, you know. So he is making big mysteries. But is all pretend.'

'He didn't strike me as a man who would do much pretending. Have you been talking to him? About me and Paula.'

'No, no. Well, a word or two maybe. But is nothing, nothing.'

Zalski had obviously taken a pretty big cargo of vodka on board, and Brady was afraid it had loosened his tongue. There was no telling how much he had let slip to Malkowicz and others. And how far could one trust any of them? He would certainly not have trusted Malkowicz further than he could see him; and maybe not even as far as that. But what could he do about it?

Zalski gave him another slap on the shoulder. 'Cheer up, my friend. Tomorrrow everything is good. We go like hell. You see.'

Which was all very fine, Brady thought, but who wanted to go like hell?

*   *   *

'Are you awake?' he said.

'Yes, Walter, I am awake.'

'What do you think of Zalski?'

'In what way?'

'Do you think he's dependable?'

'I think he is perhaps a little wild; but a good man, I am sure.'

'He may be a good man, but he talks

too much.'

'It will be all right, Walter.'

'Are you going with me, Paula?'

'Do you really want me to?'

'You know I want you to. Don't you want to be with me?'

He heard her give a sigh. 'Sometimes I think I would like to be with you always.'

His hand moved in the darkness, caressing her. 'Do you truly mean that?'

'I mean it, Walter. Truly.'

He thought about it and could see all manner of reasons why it was not on. But at the same time he was thinking of the way it might be. She would have to come to England, of course, but that could be done; somehow or another it could be arranged. And he would have to find a job, a good steady job with none of this damned undercover work on the side; never any more of that either for him or for her. God, it would be marvellous; it would be the most marvellous thing in the world. And why not? For Pete's sake, why not?

'You are saying nothing, Walter. What are you thinking?'

'I'm thinking I may be falling in love with you, Paula,' he said. 'Will you go with me tomorrow?'

'Yes,' she said, 'I will go with you. And maybe soon you will be certain.'

CHAPTER NINE

ODER-NEISSE

They breakfasted late. Paula had been out for a walk earlier, explaining that she felt the need for some fresh air. Brady had suggested going with her, but she had insisted that that would not be wise and he had remained in the house. He had been relieved when she returned.

The guests of the previous evening appeared to have departed, but the signs of their revelry remained; there were empty bottles, fragments of uneaten food, cigarette-ends, a certain staleness in the air of the room where they had talked and sung and danced. Brady thought of Malkowicz counting money in his bank—or perhaps engaged in other, less harmless activities. He wished there had been no party, no guests. Why had it had to be that particular evening? Surely Relke might have arranged matters better.

Zalski appeared to be none the worse for his drinking; he ate heartily and seemed to be suffering from no hangover; which was surprising, to say the least. An old woman prepared and served the meal. Brady had not seen her before, and he was not sure whether she lived in the house or just came in to do the chores.

Relke came in briefly to see how things were going and then walked out again. Zalski told them that Relke owned the house and eked out a living by letting rooms. He had been an officer in the Polish army but had come down in the world.

'And all those people who were here last night. They were lodgers?'

'Not all, no. Some.'

'Where are they now?'

'They go to work. Some. Some still in bed. Not feel so good. You know.' Zalski put a finger to his forehead and laughed. 'Too much vodka.'

Brady thought a boarding-house seemed a strange rendezvous to choose, but he was rapidly becoming convinced that the Poles were strange people, a bit crazy. There was no accounting for anything they did. And maybe it was as safe there as anywhere else; it was hardly the kind of place the police would be likely to search for spies. Unless, of course, they were tipped off. Again he thought of Malkowicz and again felt a touch of uneasiness.

It was getting on for eleven o'clock when they left. There was a two-ton, high-sided lorry parked in a yard at the back of the house, and the three of them climbed into the cab, the girl sitting in the middle and Zalski at the wheel. Zalski was wearing a black leather jacket over the same check shirt he had had on the previous evening.

'Not like Rolls-Royce car,' he said. 'But will be getting you there, I think.'

'Where?' Brady asked.

'You wait, you see.'

That seemed to be the story of his life, Brady thought. Nobody ever told him anything.

Zalski had made no objection to taking Paula along; in fact he seemed very happy to have her join them, not bothered in the least that it should not have been in the plan. Brady had already formed the opinion that Zalski was of an independent nature and was not much concerned with authority of any kind. That could be a good trait, but on the other hand it could land them in trouble. He just hoped the occasion would not arise when Zalski felt the urge to act rashly rather than circumspectly.

As far as he could judge, they were travelling roughly in a westward direction. The lorry had been around a good many years and it had not been used with kindness. There was a lot of noise in the cab and such a strong odour of petrol that Brady wondered a shade uneasily whether it might not be leaking out somewhere. The road was reasonably good for the first forty or fifty kilometres and Zalski kept the lorry hammering along at a useful speed. They crossed a river with a lot of boats and barges on it, and Paula remarked that it was the Odra.

'Is that the same as the Oder?' Brady asked; and she said yes, it was the same river.

Something gave a click in his head and a voice seemed to whisper: 'Oder-Neisse line.' He wondered whether there was any significance in that, and he hoped not, because if there was he wanted to get out and go home. But of course there was no possibility of doing that, so he just sat tight and said nothing.

A few kilometres farther on Zalski swung the lorry off to the right on to a minor road, and after that the roads seemed to become more and more minor and the going more and more rugged. They were well into the country, with nothing but tiny villages and little fields laid out in a kind of strip pattern. They looked like peasant holdings and Brady remembered what Paula had told him—that most of the Polish farmers stoutly resisted regimentation into collectives and still cultivated their own small bits of land for private profit. It was not the Communist way, but it had the great advantage of producing the goods. There were some tractors at work, but the horse was still very much in evidence.

It was early in the afternoon when they drove down a narrow, bumpy lane and came to an old farmhouse and some outbuildings. Zalski stopped the lorry and switched off the engine.

'We stop here a little,' he said. 'We eat, rest,

125

then we are going on.'

'What place is this?' Brady asked.

'Is where I am born. My father's farm. We are welcome here. You see.'

He was right about the welcome, though Brady guessed it was chiefly for him. For his sake there would probably have been hospitality for anyone he chose to bring with him.

The mother was the first to appear; she had heard the lorry and came out of the house as they were stepping down from the cab. She was a stout, middle-aged woman dressed in a coarse blouse and skirt and with a head-scarf covering her hair. She embraced Zalski and then looked shyly at Paula and Brady as he introduced them. These introductions had scarcely been completed when the man came out of a barn on the other side of the yard where the lorry had stopped. He had a bony, weather-beaten face that was an older edition of his son's, and there were bits of hay adhering to his clothes. He, too, greeted Zalski with every sign of pleasure and the introductions were repeated.

Zalski spoke to the woman, and he must have been telling her that they were hungry and rather pressed for time, for she went back into the house and began to prepare a meal at once. They followed her into a kitchen with whitewashed walls, a low ceiling and some heavy wooden furniture. There was an oil-lamp hanging from a beam and an old-fashioned cooking-stove on the left with some pots and pans standing on it.

The woman busied herself in the preparation of the meal while Zalski drew the man on one side and spoke to him in a low, confidential tone of voice. The man nodded once or twice but said little; occasionally he glanced at Brady and the girl, and Brady thought he detected a certain uneasiness in the glances. He had the feeling that what Zalski was telling his father was not altogether to the older man's liking, though he was not making any apparent protest. After a few minutes he and Zalski went out of the house.

A little later Zalski returned alone, and he and the other two sat down to the food which the woman had placed on the table. It was a simple but substantial meal—a heated-up stew, home-baked bread and cider to drink. The woman did not sit down with them but busied herself with various tasks about the kitchen.

'She is shy,' Zalski confided. 'Is not often there are guests coming to the house, and one not Polish.'

'Perhaps she wonders why we are here,' Brady said.

'Perhaps.'

'I wonder a little myself.'

Zalski smiled but said nothing.

When they stepped out of the house Brady saw at once that the lorry had been moved; it had been backed into the barn.

'It has to be loaded,' Zalski explained. 'And for the next part of the journey you must be riding on the back. Will not be far.'

Brady was puzzled, but he made no comment. They went into the barn and found Zalski's father there. There were some crates of cabbages and cauliflowers stacked on one side, as well as a number of sacks which might have contained potatoes or other vegetables. On the lorry, close up against the cab, was already one fairly large crate with an open end. The crate was empty. Brady felt that he knew what this crate was for, and it was certainly not cabbages.

'You want me to get inside that?'

'For not long,' Zalski said. He turned to Paula. 'You, too, please. Is best, I think.'

'Why?' Brady asked.

'Is best you are not being seen.'

'Why mustn't we be seen?'

Zalski did not answer that, but Paula said: 'Please don't argue about it. Do as he says.'

With Zalski's help she climbed on to the back of the lorry. Brady still considered he was entitled to an explanation but decided not to press the matter. He climbed up without any assistance from Zalski.

There was just room in the crate for them to sit side by side with their backs to the cab and their knees drawn up, the suitcase at their feet. It was a position that was not going to be very comfortable if the ride proved to be at all long. But Zalski had promised that it would not be and they had to take his word for that.

As soon as they were inside Zalski and his father set about loading the other crates and the sacks of vegetables. They worked quickly and within a few minutes the hiding-place of the two passengers was effectively concealed by the rest of the load. Brady heard the tail-board go up, and a short while after that the engine started and the lorry began to move. He was pressed very close to the girl and every time the lorry gave a lurch the pressure was increased.

'Well,' he said, 'it's certainly cosy.'

She made no comment. Perhaps she found it a little too cosy. There was a smell of vegetables reminiscent of a greengrocer's shop, and though Zalski had thoughtfully provided a folded sack for them to sit on, it was not much of a cushion and tended to get harder as time went on. Nevertheless, in spite of the discomfort, Brady had a feeling of drowsiness, which was probably the effect of the meal he had eaten. He was half dozing when the thought came into his mind that this was not the first time he had travelled in a crate with an attractive girl as a companion.

There had been that time in Russia in the back of a big articulated lorry; but the crate then had been a lot bigger and the girl had been Linda Manning. It had, too, been a longer journey than this was likely to be, and they had gone clean across the frontier into Finland. This time, of course, they would not be crossing any frontier.

Or would they?

Suddenly he was not feeling drowsy any more; he was very wide awake. 'Oh God!' he said. 'Not that!'

The girl turned her head. It was pretty dark in the crate, but there was a little light getting through and he could see the vague outline of her face.

'Not what?' she asked.

'The Oder-Neisse line.'

'What about the Oder-Neisse line?'

'That's the border, isn't it?'

'Well, yes,' she said.

'And we're going to cross it, aren't we?'

She put a hand on his arm. 'Now don't start getting upset again, Walter. Everything is going to be all right. Jan knows what he's doing.'

'Oh, I'm sure he does. The point is I'm not at all sure I like what he's doing.'

'He is only carrying out his instructions.'

'I'm getting to be a bit sick of those instructions.'

'Why do you always have to make such

a fuss?'

'I want to get out,' Brady said.

He thought of making an attempt to break out of the crate, but it would have meant pushing aside all the other crates and sacks that were piled round it, and he was not at all sure he could do that. So he was still thinking about it and doing nothing when the lorry came to a halt and then began to advance in fits and starts. He knew what that meant—they were in a traffic queue at some kind of road-block or checkpoint, and it took no great powers of deduction to conclude that they were at the border. He could hear men's voices and a thumping noise like a pile-driver at work, and then they were moving steadily forward again and there was the sound you get when you go over a bridge. This is it, he thought; this is the Oder or maybe the Neisse and we're right bang on top of it. Nice going, Brady.

He felt Paula's hand on his arm again, gripping it a little hard, as though to give him encouragement. And he certainly needed encouraging; he needed just about all she could do for him in that line and maybe more besides. And then the lorry stopped again and he thought her hand trembled slightly, so maybe she was in need of a bit of encouragement herself; maybe she was not quite as confident that everything would work out all right as she had pretended. He remembered that she had not been bound to come with him this far; she had done it for his sake, because he had asked her to, and he ought to be grateful. So he put his hand on hers by way of showing his appreciation of what she had done, and after that they just sat and waited.

There were some more voices, and now and then an engine would start up and a vehicle would grind past in low gear, presumably going the other way; but the thumping noise had faded, so it looked as though the pile-driver had been working on the other side of the river. Then suddenly a voice shouted something and it was so close that Brady gave a start and felt the grip on his arm tighten. He guessed that somebody had climbed on to the lorry and was taking a look at the load, and he just hoped they would not see anything suspicious. But nothing was shifted and a few moments later they were on the move again and Zalski was going up through the gears and the speed was increasing.

The girl removed her hand from his arm, and when she spoke there was no hint in her voice that she had experienced any uneasiness.

'You see. It was all right.'

'I got the impression for a moment back there that you thought it might not be.'

'One can never be quite certain. There is always a possibility that things may go wrong.'

'You didn't tell me that before.'

'I didn't want to alarm you.'

'They didn't make much of a search.'

'Why should they? Jan often comes this way with farm produce. They wouldn't suspect him of carrying anything illegal.'

It sounded reasonable. All these Iron Curtain countries were part of Comecon, weren't they? All members of the same club. Presumably stuff like farm produce went across from one to another with the minimum of formality. It was not like trying to cart something over to the West; there you really would have trouble.

Half an hour later Zalski stopped the lorry and they could hear him shifting some of the load to let them out. They squeezed through the gap he had made and scrambled down on to the side of the road. The daylight was already fading and the coolness of evening was in the air. Zalski appeared to have got the lorry off the main road and everything was very quiet. There was a small wood on one side and farmland on the other.

'You like to be stretching your legs?'

Brady was trying to get the stiffness out of his knees and his back; he had been sitting in a cramped position for too long; a bit longer and he would have needed lifting out with a crane. Paula seemed less affected; she had not had to fold herself up quite so much.

'You ride in front again now,' Zalski said. 'Nobody is stopping us again.'

'What country are we in?' Brady asked. As if he didn't know!

'Germany,' Zalski said.

'East Germany?'

Zalski laughed. 'No Polish frontier with West Germany. You look at map.'

'Damn you,' Brady said. 'Why didn't you tell me? I haven't got a visa for East Germany.'

Zalski was unconcerned. 'Why you wanting a visa? You are here. Visa—' He snapped his fingers, dismissing such an unnecessary formality. 'Now we are going on. Ready?'

They climbed into the cab and Zalski started the engine. Brady just hoped he avoided getting himself involved in a road accident; that would really set things up. But Zalski was driving with care and there was very little traffic. He had switched on the lights and with an overcast sky night seemed to have closed in very rapidly.

'How much further do we have to go?' Brady asked. He had no way of telling in what direction they were going; all he knew was that it certainly was not east.

'Not very far,' Zalski said.

They drove on for a time with nobody saying a word, the lorry making all the noise. Then Zalski said: 'We are getting followed.'

CHAPTER TEN

LITTLE SPY

'Followed!' Brady said.

Zalski had made the statement very calmly, in an ordinary matter-of-fact tone of voice, as though he had been making nothing more important than an announcement of the time of day. But it was certainly a lot more important than that. If he was right and they were in fact being followed, they were in trouble, no doubt about it; maybe bad trouble.

'How do you know?'

'Something is behind. Car, I think. You see lights?' Brady put his head out of the window and looked back along the road. The lights of another vehicle some distance behind were indeed visible. He drew his head in again.

'You see?' Zalski asked.

'There is something behind, certainly. But what makes you think it's following us? This is a public road, isn't it? Anyone can use it.'

'They are not catching up. I am slowing speed; I am slowing very much. They are still staying behind. So I am asking myself why. Why are they not catching us? Why not passing when I am going so slow?'

'Maybe the driver is a nervous man,' Brady suggested. 'Maybe he doesn't like overtaking.'

It sounded very thin; he had no belief in it himself, and Zalski had no belief in it, either.

'Okay,' Zalski said. 'So I stop. Then we see.'

He pulled the lorry to a halt by the side of the road. Brady looked out of the window. The headlights of the vehicle behind were obscured by a bend in the road, but a moment later they appeared again. They came on for a little way, then stopped and approached no closer. They went out suddenly, only the glimmer of the sidelights remaining visible.

'What you thinking now?' Zalski asked.

'I'm thinking you're right,' Brady said. 'See what happens when you go on again.'

What happened was precisely what he had expected: when the lorry got on the move again the driver of the other vehicle gave it a bit of time to draw clear, then settled down once more to the pursuit, never making any attempt to overtake but always there on the tail.

'I don't understand,' Paula said. 'If they're the police why don't they get in front and stop us?'

'I think they are wanting we lead them some place,' Zalski said.

Brady thought Zalski was probably right. If the East German security people knew what kind of business Zalski was on they would most certainly want to know where he was going. But that presupposed something else; that they had been tipped off regarding the lorry. And that in turn raised the question: who had done the tipping off? The name that immediately sprang into his mind was Malkowicz.

'Somebody must have talked,' he said.

Zalski agreed. 'Is possible.'

'I'd call it probable. I'd call it a dead certainty.'

'Maybe.'

'And I'd say it was friend Malkowicz.'

'There is no proof of that,' Paula said.

'No proof. But he'd be top on my list of suspects.'

'No use to be arguing about that,' Zalski said. 'We got this damn car behind. We better be doing something.'

'What can we do?'

Zalski made no answer to this question. They came to a place where another road cut in from the left; the following vehicle was possibly a quarter of a mile behind, possibly more. Zalski stopped the lorry, put it quickly into reverse and backed into the other road. Then he switched off the lights.

Brady supposed Zalski was counting on the pursuers driving straight past without spotting the lorry, but for his own part he had no great hopes of eluding them by this simple manoeuvre. However, it very quickly became apparent that Zalski had no such thing in mind, for he immediately put the lorry into forward gear again, drove out on to the other road and turned right, so that they were now heading in the direction from which they had come.

The road was illuminated by the headlamps of the pursuing vehicle, which was now close enough to be identifiable as a big saloon car. Zalski put his foot down on the accelerator and the lorry gathered speed, solidly straddling the crown of the narrow road and heading straight for the car.

Brady had known all along that it was only a matter of time before Zalski did something really crazy, and now he was doing it. What did he want? A head-on collision? Well, that was certainly what he was going to get. Brady wanted to yell at him to stop, to pull over to the side of the road, but nothing came out. And there was no time anyway; the lorry and the car were closing at the sum of their individual speeds and it added up to quite a bit, even if neither was travelling really fast. They had not been very far apart at the start of the exercise, and it was all happening very rapidly and not giving anyone much time to take avoiding action. What action there was in that line was taken by the driver of the car. Zalski just drove straight on with his foot still on the accelerator.

The car-driver was a shade too slow in his reactions. When he started to brake and pull off to the right it was already too late to avoid the collision entirely; what he did succeed in doing was to turn the head-on impact into a glancing one. Zalski, still driving his lorry furiously along the crown of the road, hit the car half-way along the left-hand side with a grinding crunch and squeal of metal on metal. Brady felt the shock of it, and the lorry veered to the right and hit the verge and ran bumping and banging along it for a while before Zalski had it back on the road. He switched the lights on, drove on a little way further, found another place to turn, and got the vehicle once again pointed in the direction in which it had originally been heading.

'You're surely not going back there,' Brady said. It looked like asking for more trouble.

'Is way we bloody got to went,' Zalski said.

There was no arguing with a man who used that kind of logic in that kind of English, so Brady gave him his head. He would have taken it anyway.

The headlights revealed the car while the lorry was still picking up speed. The car was lying on its side a few feet off the road and there was some gouged earth where it had ploughed a way through. There was one man standing beside it; in fact he seemed to be leaning on it, as if he needed some support. How many others there might have been in the car was anybody's guess, but however many there had been, they were still in it, and maybe injured or even dead.

And then Brady saw that though the man

who had got out might not have been in the best of shape, he was in good enough shape to aim a gun, and he was in fact doing just that. It was a pistol of some kind, and he was holding it with both hands and pointing it at the cab of the approaching lorry.

The clever thing would have been to get down below the level of the windscreen. Brady knew that. The girl probably knew it, too. Neither of them did the clever thing; they sat where they were and kept their eyes on the man with the pistol. He took a shot at them when the lorry was about fifteen yards away; the crack of the pistol was audible above the racket of the engine and there was a thin whining sound which might have been the bullet skidding off a bit of the metalwork. And then there was another crack and a tinkle of breaking glass, and one of the headlights went out.

They were level with the car by that time, and Brady caught a glimpse of the man as they hammered past. He was a stocky individual in a short leather coat with a belt round the waist. He was not wearing a hat and his hair was cropped short; it was very fair hair and his face looked pale when the light caught it. Brady got an impression of anger, even of hatred; but it was a fleeting vision, like a face glimpsed through a carriage window when two trains pass, seen for a moment and then lost. There was a sound of one more shot, but they were past by then and going fast, and one thing was certain: the car would not be on their tail again. Zalski had solved that problem.

'Is damn good fun, you think?' he asked.

'Depends what you mean by fun.' For his part Brady preferred something a shade less exciting. This might be all right for the kind of people who enjoyed playing Russian roulette, but that had never had much appeal for him. 'What puzzles me is how they managed to pick us up. Do you think they tailed us all the way from the border?'

Zalski shook his head. 'No. They are getting on to us later. After you don't get in the box any more.'

'But how could they do that? They wouldn't know which way you were going.'

'True,' Zalski said, and he seemed to be rather thoughtful for a while. Then suddenly he applied the brakes and brought the lorry to a stop.

'What now?' Brady asked.

'Now I think we are taking a little look around.'

'Looking for what?'

'For damage maybe.'

They all got out and all looked round for damage. There was not much that was new—a few more dents in the front wing where it had hit the car, the broken headlamp, a gouge mark left by the bullet that had ricochetted, nothing else of note.

Zalski took a torch out of the cab and started peering under the chassis, which seemed to be taking things a little far, Brady thought. What did he expect to find under there? Termites?

Whatever Zalski did or did not expect to find, his search did not prove altogether unproductive. He was looking under the tail when he found it. He gave a tug and it came away in his hand. He held it out to show it to the others.

'We got extra passenger.'

Brady looked at the thing lying on the palm of Zalski's hand. It was circular in shape and slightly flattened, rather like a woman's compact. He had not seen one before, but he guessed what it was.

'A bleeper.'

Zalski nodded. 'Little spy under the tail. Is how they are getting on to us so good. No need for following all the way; just listen to little blips.'

'But who could have fixed it? And where?' Paula said.

'Somebody at border. When I don't looking somebody creeping under tail and fixing this. Is magnetic, so is sticking to metal.'

'So there must have been a tip-off,' Brady said. 'That proves it.' He still thought it was Malkowicz who had given the information; but, as the girl had said, there was no proof of that.

He looked again at the small object in Zalski's hand. Presumably it was still sending out its signal, which might still be picked up; there was no certainty that the wrecked car had been the only one in contact. Moreover, there could be little doubt that the man who had shot at them would be taking some kind of action; he might already be getting into touch with headquarters and giving a report of what had happened. Then the hunt would really be on. Brady's sense of elation at getting away from one lot of pursuers gave way to a sick feeling in the stomach. They were still in trouble and they were likely to be in more; because even if they managed to wriggle out of the present sticky situation, how the devil were they going to get back across the border into Poland now that all the security forces were on the alert? And besides, what good would it be to him personally to get back into Poland, anyway? They would never let him out again now. He hadn't a hope of walking on board a ship in Gdansk and getting a passage back to England. This time he was really and truly in the soup.

'Don't you think you'd better get rid of that thing?' he said. And if his voice sounded sour that was natural enough, because that was the way he felt. 'Unless you're thinking of keeping it as a souvenir.'

'No,' Zalski said. 'I think I don't keep it.' He lifted his hand and threw the little spy into the

143

darkness. 'Come. We go now. Sooner, better.'

They climbed back into the cab and Zalski got the lorry going again.

'What are your plans now? Brady asked.

'No change,' Zalski said. He appeared surprised that such a question should be asked. 'We are going same place we would have went before. What else?'

Brady had no alternative suggestion to make. It was all mess but he supposed it would be no more of a mess if they went through with the original plan. He subsided into a morose silence and gave himself up to undiluted depression. The lorry rattled on and Zalski was still keeping to minor roads on which there was not a great deal of traffic. He seemed to have a very good knowledge of that part of the country, for he never showed any hesitation and never once referred to a map. They came to a small village, but there were few people about. They went through it, and there was a length of straight road lying ahead and everything appeared to be going well until a policeman on a motor-cycle overtook them and signalled to them to stop.

Zalski swore and Brady would not have been altogether surprised if he had driven on in spite of the signal, and possibly straight at the policeman if he had been fool enough to get in the way. But if any such idea had been in Zalski's mind he controlled the impulse and pulled the lorry to a halt.

The motor-cycle policeman left his machine by the side of the road and walked back towards the lorry, and Brady was thinking it had not taken long for the message to get through, so maybe all the police in the area had been warned to be on the lookout for any two-tonner with a Polish registration and a load of vegetables. Which was a happy thought.

'Leave talking to me,' Zalski said.

Brady was quite prepared to do that. He was not sure about Paula, but he himself was not much better at the German language than he was at Polish, and he had no desire to try to make himself understood by a German policeman who, as he could see, had a pistol in a holster on his belt. He was rather surprised that the pistol was still in the holster and not in the man's hand, but he knew that this might be only a temporary state of affairs.

The policeman reached the cab and said something to Zalski. Zalski answered in an easy tone of voice. The policeman spoke again; he was a young man and he seemed relaxed. Zalski opened the door and got out of the cab.

He said: 'Is just tail light is going out. No trouble.'

He walked to the rear of the lorry with the policeman keeping him company to have a look at the faulty light.

Brady said: 'I think it is trouble all the same.

145

That policeman is going to ask questions.'

'Then we shall have to answer them,' Paula said.

'I'm not supposed to be in Germany.'

'He may not ask about that. He may only be interested in traffic regulations.'

'Cops are interested in anything illegal.'

'Now you're worrying again, Walter.'

'You bet your sweet life I am,' Brady said. 'And I have reason to be.'

The policeman came back with Zalski and they went round to the front of the lorry and looked at the broken headlamp. The policeman seemed to be interested in that, so maybe there was something illegal about having a headlamp shot to pieces, and it was not going to be much use explaining that it was a government agent who had done the shooting. Zalski and the policeman seemed to be having quite a long discussion as they stood by the radiator of the lorry, and then Zalski pulled some papers out of his pocket and showed them to the policeman, and after that he stowed them away again and the two of them came back to the cab, the policeman leading and Zalski a few paces behind. The policeman put his right hand on the door and looked at Brady and the girl and said something. He had a rather hoarse voice, which came perhaps from riding about on a motor-cycle in all weathers and at all hours of the day and night; or maybe just from smoking too many cigarettes made from Russian tobacco—or any other kind of tobacco, if it came to that.

Brady looked at the policeman and said nothing; and Zalski said: 'He is wishing to see your papers.'

Brady took his eyes off the policeman's face and looked at Zalski instead. He wanted to ask what in hell Zalski thought he should do about it, because they both knew that all the papers he had on him were not going to convince an East German policeman that he had any right to be where he was at that particular moment. But when he looked at Zalski he saw Zalski give a wink and a lopsided grin; and Zalski lifted his right hand and gave the policeman a chop on the side of the neck; and the policeman sagged at the knees and went down, so it looked as though Zalski knew his karate, or at least enough of it to fit the present emergency if nothing else.

'Now,' Zalski said, 'lend me hand to getting him off the bloody road. Quick now.'

Brady got out of the cab on the other side and ran round the front of the lorry. Zalski had his hands under the policeman's armpits and was already starting to drag him across the road. Brady took the legs and together they carried the unconscious man to the grass verge. There was an overgrown ditch with a little water in the bottom. 'Now,' Zalski said, and they heaved the policeman into the ditch.

He lay there on his back very peacefully, soaking up some of the water and out of sight of anyone passing on the road.

Zalski ran and fetched the motor-cycle and pushed it into the ditch too—just to keep him company. A car came up as they were getting back into the lorry. It went past without even slowing.

'Now we better do some cracking,' Zalski said.

His idea of cracking was to push the lorry along at a speed that was suited neither to its age nor the condition of the road. It had been noisy enough in the cab before; now it was deafening. Brady wondered whether Zalski had ever had any ambition to be a racing driver; he might have done well at the job, for it certainly took no little driving skill to keep the lorry on the road at the speed at which it was going and with only one headlamp in working order. But he hoped there was not too much further to go, because you needed luck as well as skill at this game, and the luck might not hold out indefinitely.

In fact it held out for about ten kilometres; then it gave way and the lighting failed completely. It could scarcely have happened at a worse place; they were coming up to a pretty sharp bend in the road and suddenly there was nothing ahead but a blank screen; just utter blackness, made all the blacker by the abrupt transition from light to dark.

Brady heard Zalski swearing, and he must have taken his foot off the accelerator and stood hard on the brake pedal. He had been going into the bend much too fast for safety anyway, and now he was being forced to guess just where it was without being able to see a thing. He could certainly not bring the lorry to a halt before it got there.

For a moment Brady thought Zalski might have got his calculations right, but then there was the very devil of a bump and he knew that Zalski most surely had not. Immediately afterwards there was a splitting, rending sound and he guessed that they had gone through a fence. And then the front of the lorry dipped and it was rolling down a pretty steep slope and he wondered what it was going to hit when it got to the bottom. This is it, he thought; this is really and truly it, the end of the ride. So damn Zalski and damn Turner and damn the whole rotten business.

He tried to find something to hang on to, but nothing came to hand; and if ever there had been a time when he could have used a seat-belt, this was undoubtedly it. But there was no seat-belt either, so that when the jolt came he just felt himself being thrown forward, felt something give him one hell of a crack on the head, and then felt nothing more.

CHAPTER ELEVEN

MOLE'S LIFE

It was the girl he saw first when he regained consciousness. He was lying in a bed and she was looking down at him. He remembered the lorry going off the road and nothing after that. He had no idea where he was or how he came to be in the bed.

'Paula,' he said. His mouth felt dry and he had some difficulty in articulating clearly; it was like pushing the word through a lot of packed cobwebs.

She stooped and kissed him, and he rather liked that. She could do that as often as she wished.

'I suppose,' he said, still with that mouthful of cobweb getting in the way of clear speech, 'there must be some explanation.'

'Explanation?'

'Of how I come to be here.' He turned his head a little, but his neck felt stiff and the movement was not accomplished without some pain; not bad pain but enough to discourage any vigorous action. He could see, however, that he was in a rather small room with no window and a minimum of furniture; a clinically clean room with white walls.

'How much do you remember?' the

150

girl asked.

'I remember the lights failing and the lorry getting out of control; crashing through a fence or something and falling into a kind of pit. After that I seem to have blacked out.'

'You had a rather bad knock on the head. You've been unconscious for over two days.'

'Two days!' He made a movement to sit up and felt a stab of pain in his left side.

She put a hand on his shoulder. 'Now don't get excited. You're going to be quite all right. They had to do an operation, but—'

'Operation!'

'Nothing serious. They'll be taking the stitches out very shortly.'

'So this is a hospital?'

'No; not exactly.'

'What, then?'

'It's the place we were trying to get to when the accident occurred.'

'So how did I get here? You're not saying you carried me?'

'Of course not. Luckily Jan and I were not much hurt; just a bit shaken and bruised, nothing worse. We got you out of the lorry and I stayed with you while Jan went off and found somewhere to make a telephone call. Fortunately he didn't have very far to go.'

'And then?'

'Then they sent a car and brought us in.'

'I see. And is Jan here now?'

'Yes.'

151

'Has he abandoned the lorry?'

'That was necessary. Even if it could have been salvaged it would not have been safe to use it again.'

'No; I can see that. It's become too well known.'

She said: 'Plans have been altered, I'm afraid. Jan was to have taken you back to Poland the way you came in, but of course that's impossible now. We shall have to cross the border somewhere else and in some other way.'

'You make it sound so easy,' Brady said. 'But it isn't going to be easy, is it? They'll be on the watch for us. They know we're in Germany and they'll be pretty certain we'll try to get out. What chance do you think we'll stand?'

'There are always ways of doing these things.'

He did not believe it; he just did not believe it would be possible for them to slip back into Poland, not with all the border guards on the alert to pick them up. And even if they got into Poland he still had to find a way of getting back to England, and he could not for the life of him see how that was to be done. For the present he was all right, apart from a stiff neck, a throbbing headache and a pain in the left side, but when he tried to peer into the future it looked black indeed. And he still had no idea why he was there.

He asked the girl if she knew the answer, but she shook her head. 'No; I don't know anything about that.'

'So they haven't let you into the secret?'

'No.'

He was not sure he believed her, but she could have been telling the truth. He wondered whether Zalski knew; but why would they confide in him any more than in Paula? Whoever they were.

And that story of his being knocked out for two days by a blow on the head—he was not sure he believed that, either. He was seeing clearly enough and he had no more than this slight headache, so obviously there had been no concussion; it would surely not have cleared up so quickly. But why then had he been unconscious for so long? Unless they had squirted some drug into him to keep him quiet. Well, there was nothing sinister in that if they were going to operate on him, was there? Maybe not. All the same he would have liked to know a bit more about what was going on. There was still too much groping about in the dark. And this room; it was like a cell. Why were there no windows?

He asked the girl.

'Because it is underground,' she said.

It seemed as good a reason as any.

He was going to ask her some more questions, but the door opened and a man walked in. He looked, Brady thought, like the chairman of a prosperous company; very well dressed in a dark suit and black shoes; very well groomed, with a kind of newly-scrubbed appearance; thick-rimmed glasses supported by a wide, slightly flattened nose.

'Ah,' he said, 'so the patient is awake.' He walked over to the bed and look down at Brady. 'How do you feel, Mr Storey?'

'Foul,' Brady said.

The man chuckled softly. 'That at least is honest. Permit me to introduce myself. I am Dr Leber.'

'So I'm your patient?'

'For the present, yes.'

'Did you operate on me?'

'That is so.'

'What was wrong?'

'Nothing serious.' It was what Paula had said. It was probably what she had been told. He sensed a conspiracy to play the thing down and keep him happy.

He refused to be made happy. 'It must have been serious enough to require an operation.'

'Some slight damage to the rib. It seemed wise to take the necessary measures. I am glad to say there were no complications. A very simple operation in fact. Soon you will be up and about again.'

'And away from here?'

Leber gave a faint smile. 'Naturally. You would hardly wish to stay indefinitely.'

'Frankly,' Brady said, 'I didn't wish to come.'

Dr Leber chuckled again; he seemed to think it was a joke. To him perhaps it was.

*　　*　　*

He found it tedious lying in the bed in the windowless room. It was most tedious of all when Paula was not there. He was attended by a man in a white coat who was apparently a male nurse but who spoke no English. There was also a wispy little man in an ill-fitting suit who occasionally came with Dr Leber and sat silently on a chair while the doctor talked. Leber did not introduce him, indeed acted as though he had not been there. Brady asked Paula whether she knew who this man was. She did not. Later he asked Zalski, who was still around, and Zalski said the man's name was Schmidt.

'He is metal man.'

'Metal man?'

'He is knowing about metals. Very much he is knowing about metals, I think.'

'You mean he's a metallurgist?'

'Maybe.'

'Who told you this?'

'Somebody. Maybe not true neither. Just damn lies, maybe.'

Brady got the impression that Zalski was clamming up. Perhaps he thought he had already said more than he should have done. But what would a metallurgist be doing there?

Maybe Zalski had got it all wrong anyway.

He was glad when Dr Leber allowed him to get up, though at first his legs felt as weak as a couple of sticks of boiled asparagus. He had had the stitches taken out of his side and Leber said it was coming along very nicely.

'So I'll soon be able to go?'

'Yes,' Leber said. 'Very soon now.'

Brady wondered whether he knew just how difficult that was going to be. But of course he did; he knew the score; he had to.

At first he was confined to the room, but when he had become more used to walking he was allowed more freedom. There was a lounge, with bookcases and a television set. Sometimes he watched television with Paula and Zalski, but the programmes were uninteresting and were marred by poor reception. He might have done some reading if there had been any English books, but there were not.

He wondered about Turner. Did Turner know his agent had walked into trouble? And if he knew, was it bothering him? Brady doubted whether he was losing any sleep over it. And Linda—was she worrying? Maybe. Just a little, maybe. But not as much as he himself was, that was for sure; nobody else could be worrying as much as that.

It was a mole's life, always underground. He had not had a glimpse of daylight since his arrival and had no idea what the place looked like on the surface. At this lower level there appeared to be everything necessary to sustain life; it was a self-contained, self-sufficient unit; hygienic and characterless and utterly depressing. He asked Paula what it was like above ground, but she could tell him very little.

'It was dark when we arrived. There's a house, very old, I think, and it's surrounded by trees. As soon as we got here we were brought straight down to this basement.'

'Haven't you been out since?'

'No; it is not allowed. Dr Leber says that for reasons of security we must stay down here.'

'So Jan hasn't been out, either?'

'No.'

'How does he like that?'

'He doesn't. He's impatient to be away. But of course we have to wait until you are fit to travel. Anyway, the longer we wait the safer it is likely to be; they may not be quite so much on the alert for us.'

'I wouldn't count a lot on that,' Brady said. 'Have you worked out any new plan for getting across the border?'

'We have thought of something.'

'Do I get told about it?'

'Later. There is no hurry. Just try to get fit.'

He wondered how she expected him to set about doing that. The healing process was not going to be pushed along any faster by virtue of anything he might do.

The odd thing was that even now he knew

nothing regarding the reason why he had been sent there. He had asked Dr Leber, and Leber had simply given a shake of the head and said it was none of his business. Brady had then asked whose business it was, and Leber had said he really couldn't say. It took a bit of swallowing; Brady would have wagered Dr Leber had a very good idea of what was going on. So apparently he was just being secretive. Like everyone else concerned in the matter. But eventually they would have to dish out a little information; they couldn't keep him in the dark for ever, because he was the agent, willing or unwilling, who had been sent out from London to pick something up. At least, he supposed that was the object of the exercise, since he sure as hell failed to see any other. So what was it to be? A roll of microfilm? A coded letter? A verbal message to be carried back in his head? Why were they so reluctant to confide in him? They would have to do so in the end; they must know that. Where was the risk? They had him there, safely cooped up; nothing was going to leak out. Still, if they wanted to play it this way there was nothing he could do about it. Except wait.

'I'd like to make love to you,' he said.

She gave a smile. 'I don't think you're quite in condition for that yet.'

'You might be surprised.'

'Perhaps. But I don't think it would help to

get you fit, do you? And that, after all, is what we are all waiting for.'

He had to admit that she had a case. She was probably as eager to leave the mole-run as he was. 'What will you do when you get back to Poland?'

'I don't know.' For a moment there was a worried frown puckering her forehead.

'Will you go back to the Zoppotski?'

'I don't think so.'

He could see how that might be difficult now, and he said quickly: 'Come to England with me.'

It seemed to take her by surprise. 'To England!'

'Does it sound so bad?'

'What exactly are you asking me?' she said.

'I'm asking you to marry me. What did it sound like to you?'

'That is what it sounded like to me, Walter.'

He would have to get her out of the habit of calling him that; he was not inviting her to become Mrs Walter Storey but Mrs Stephen Brady; but it was not yet the time for telling her so.

'And what do you say? Does the idea have any attraction for you?'

She kissed him. 'It has much attraction, but there are surely many obstacles in the way.'

'We can get over them.'

'Perhaps.'

'I promise you.'

'Ah, no,' she said; 'don't make any promises, Walter. You may not be able to keep them.'

'I love you, Paula.'

'So you are certain now?'

'I am certain now.'

'Well,' she said, 'we will talk about it.'

He had to be content with that.

*   *   *

'You may get dressed now,' Dr Leber said.

He had given Brady a very thorough examination and had made a lot of little grunting sounds which might have meant anything.

Brady began to pull on his clothes. 'Well?'

Dr Leber peered at him through the thick-framed glasses. 'Well what?'

'Am I fit to go?'

'Oh, you are perfectly fit, perfectly.'

The incision had healed well and there was only a small scar, barely noticeable. Dr Leber had certainly done an excellent job. He still felt a twinge of pain now and then, but Leber had assured him that this was nothing to worry about; it was perfectly natural after such an operation.

'It will go away in time. Then you will be as good as new.'

'And meanwhile there is nothing more to keep me here?'

'Nothing.'

'When do you think I shall leave?'

'That is not entirely up to me. I shall, of course, make my report on your fitness to travel and you will no doubt hear very shortly what has been decided. You are impatient to be gone?'

'Well,' Brady said, 'I've no complaint to make against the accommodation, but it's not quite the place I should choose for my holidays. I'd rather like to see what kind of weather we're having.'

Leber gave the faintest of smiles. 'That is natural perhaps. But it is possible the time may come when you will wish very much you are back here.'

'That's a risk I shall have to take,' Brady said.

*   *   *

'We are to leave tomorrow evening,' Paula said.

It was the day after his medical examination. Dr Leber had apparently made his report and the decision had been reached. He was glad, yet he felt nevertheless a sudden flutter in the stomach at the thought of leaving this safe retreat for the hazards of the world outside. He had an illogical wish that they had given him just one more day—to get used to the idea.

'Are you going to tell me the plan now?'

'Yes,' she said; 'you may as well know. We shall be taken by car for the first part of the way; then we shall have to go on foot until we reach the point where we cross the Odra.'

'You mean we walk across?' It sounded crazy.

'No; there is no bridge where we shall cross. And I am afraid you will have to leave your suitcase behind; it would be too awkward carrying it.'

'So we're to swim the Oder? How wide is it? I'm not sure I can manage more than a hundred metres in my present state of health.'

She made a gesture of exasperation. 'We shall not swim. There will be a boat. It has been arranged.'

He was not altogether sold on that arrangement. Other things had been arranged and had gone wrong. But what choice had he? If he said he didn't like the plan and would they please come up with a different one they were going to be really thrilled. And what alternative plan was likely to be any better? The plain fact was, he had no right to be in East Germany at all, but now he was here it was going to be the devil getting out.

'So I'm to leave my luggage,' he said. 'Okay. And have they told you what I'm to take instead?'

She seemed puzzled. 'Instead?'

'I came here to get something. It's about time I heard what the something is, don't you

162

think? There isn't much time left.'

'Oh, that,' she said. 'Well, as a matter of fact you're not going to take anything. They've decided that after what has happened the risk would be too great.'

He stared at her. He didn't believe it; he simply did not believe it. 'You mean to say I've been through all this for nothing? You mean that after I've risked my neck, taken a bang on the head and had to have my inside patched up, I'm to be sent back empty-handed?' He felt aggrieved. They had no right to do this to him. And what was Turner going to say when he got back with nothing to show for his pains? If he ever did get back—and there was no certainty about that, too true there wasn't. Not that he gave a damn what Turner said, but it was a bit much all the same.

The girl said quietly: 'You should not forget that there are others who have also taken some risks.'

He felt ashamed at once. She for one had taken just as many risks as he had. 'I'm sorry, Paula. You're quite right. I ought not to have forgotten what you've done.'

'And Jan.'

'Jan too.' He was not so concerned about Zalski. The girl meant more to him than a thousand Zalskis.

'They have their reasons,' she said. 'You must see that.'

He could see it well enough. They knew he

163

was at risk as soon as he walked out of that damned cellar, and they were not prepared to bet on his chances of making it back to London. They preferred to wait for another courier, somebody who was not so accident prone. Well, so be it. It was funny when you came to think about it: now he never would know what it was he had come there for. Yes, that really was funny.

Not that he felt like laughing.

CHAPTER TWELVE

PLEASANT JOURNEY

It was dark when they came out of the house, and Brady saw that it was, as Paula had said, surrounded by trees. He got an impression of a gloomy old pile of building with scarcely any lights showing, and of the interior he had seen only a tile-floored passage and a chilly entrance hall. Dr Leber was there to see them off, but there was no sign of the man called Schmidt.

Dr Leber insisted on shaking hands. 'I trust you will have a pleasant journey, Mr Storey.'

Brady wondered whether the good doctor was being funny. Pleasant was about the last thing the journey was likely to be.

'I'm not asking for anything as improbable as that.'

'A journey without incident, then, shall we say?'

'I shall be very happy if it is,' Brady said.

There was a car waiting for them; it was a fairly new Wartburg saloon. The man who had acted as a male nurse was standing beside it.

'Franz will drive you,' Dr Leber said. 'He knows where to go and he is completely trustworthy.'

Brady hoped that was true. Somebody else

passing bits of information to the Secret Police was a luxury they could very well do without.

'Goodbye then, Dr Leber. Thank you for your kindness.' He wondered whether Leber expected a fee for his surgical work, but he did not suggest it. Let him send the bill to Turner.

They got into the car, he and Paula in the back, Zalski in front with Franz.

'So now,' Zalski said, 'is at last going back home. And hoping no damn trouble, don't you say?'

'I'm with you there,' Brady said.

Zalski appeared to be in good spirits, obviously glad to be on his way back to Poland and apparently with no qualms about getting there. Yet the future must surely be very dicey for him if the East German police were acting in collaboration with the Poles. In either Germany or Poland he was almost certainly liable to be arrested unless he went into hiding. And the same might be said for Paula Nowicki. So what had either of them to be cheerful about?

He spoke to the girl, softly, so that Zalski should not hear. 'You must come with me, Paula.'

She turned to him. 'I am with you, Walter.'

'I mean to England. It won't be safe for you in Poland after this.'

'That is possible,' she admitted.

'So you will come with me?'

'There is a problem, Walter.'

166

'Problem?'

'Have you thought how you are going to get back to England yourself?'

'I was hoping—'

She finished the sentence for him. 'You were hoping that there would be some emergency plan for slipping you out of the country. Is that what you mean?'

He could see no other way he was going to make it. Without help he was sunk. But why should anyone bother about him now? He was no longer of any use, so why shouldn't they let him sink?

She must have guessed what was in his mind. 'Now you are worrying, aren't you? But I will tell you—there is a plan. You will be taken care of.'

'And will you come with me?'

'That is not part of the plan.'

'We can make it a part.'

'I am not sure that would be possible.'

'Of course it would be possible. It must be. I can't leave you now. You must see that.'

'If I were to leave Poland I could never return. It would be to cut myself off from my country, my people.'

He could understand the wrench it would be for her. She must have friends, relations, of whom he knew nothing; he knew so little about her. It was asking a great deal of her to leave everything.

'Do you love me, Paula?'

There was a moment's hesitation before she replied. Then: 'Perhaps.'

'Only perhaps! You're not sure?'

'Suppose at this moment I said I am. Suppose I even believed that. Things alter with time. Suppose—'

He knew what she would have said. Suppose it didn't last, what then? And it would have been foolish to protest that there was no possibility of its not lasting. Things could go wrong, fall apart; it happened all the time.

'We will talk about it, Walter.'

'We are talking about it.'

'Later. We will talk about it later.'

He knew then that she had rejected it. He felt a stab of regret, but there was some relief mixed in there, too. It would have raised so many problems. Where would they have lived? In that scruffy little pad he rented from Mrs Groucher? He could hardly see her fitting in there. And what would they have lived on? On what he made scratching around at one thing and another? It was scarcely enough to support one person in anything like decent style. It had been a sweet dream, but dreams had a way of fading; they failed to survive the cold light of dawn. In the end you had to face the hard facts.

'You're not going to do it, are you, Paula?' he said.

She gave his hand a squeeze but said nothing. He knew what it meant: she was not going to do it.

It was raining slightly. There was a reddish glow in the sky away to the left, as though a fire were burning. But he knew it was no fire.

'What town is that?'

'Frankfurt.'

'Frankfurt is in West Germany.'

'You're thinking of Frankfurt-am-Main. This is Frankfurt-an-der-Oder.'

'You're not planning to cross there?'

'We are not going to Frankfurt,' she said.

He had not really supposed they were. It would be at some less populous place; some place where a boat might cross with a reasonable chance of being unobserved. If there was such a place.

Zalski had made a few attempts to get into conversation with Franz, but the German seemed to be a taciturn man and after a while Zalski gave it up and lapsed into silence. Paula was also silent and Brady decided to make a fourth. A certain lowering of spirits seemed to have occurred all round; even Zalski no longer appeared to be as cheerful as he had been at the start of the ride. The thin drizzle of rain was certainly not helping matters; it was a dismal sort of night, although perhaps this was to their advantage, since there might be less likelihood of their being detected.

Traffic was not heavy; an occasional car slid past, travelling in the opposite direction; nothing overtook them and they overtook nothing. Franz kept the Wartburg going at a sober speed, not pushing it, taking no risks. He knew what his job was and he obviously intended making sure that if any mishaps were to occur they could not be attributed to foolish recklessness on his part. Which was just as well.

They had been going for perhaps fifteen or twenty kilometres in this almost silent and somewhat low-spirited fashion when Franz took the car down a turning to the left on to a narrower road. They passed under an arch which appeared to be a railway bridge and a little further on took a right turn and found themselves shut in by gloomy walls of trees on both sides. The road they were now following was even narrower than the previous one and it wound in and out among the trees like a snake wriggling a way through. After about a kilometre or so of this kind of progress Franz drew the car to a halt and switched off the engine. He turned and said something to Zaiski.

Zaiski said: 'We are having to get out.'

They all got out. There was scarcely any sound in the wood apart from the steady dripping of the rain. Paula was wearing her blue raincoat and she had her shoulder-bag with her. Brady was also in a raincoat but Zalski had only his leather jacket to keep him dry.

Franz walked over to the left-hand side of

the road and Zalski went with him. They stood there talking in low tones for a while, leaving Brady and the girl by the car.

Brady said: 'I wonder what he's stopped here for. Do you know?'

'I imagine this is where he leaves us.'

'You mean he's not going all the way?'

'I don't think so.'

'A fine sort of guide that is.'

'It would not be wise for him to leave the car, and it isn't possible to drive it all the way to the boat. He is probably telling Jan where to go from here.'

'It's a sweet night to find our own way. We could wander round until morning.'

'I'm sure that will not happen.'

It was nice to know she was sure; for his part Brady had no such confidence; he thought it was a poor arrangement, altogether too damned hit or miss, with the odds on missing.

Franz and Zalski walked back to the car and Franz got into the driving seat.

Zalski said: 'He is telling me how we must be going now.'

'Well, good for him,' Brady said.

Franz had started the engine and was turning the car. They stood watching him do it. They watched him as he drove away. There were no other cars on the road. Nothing. Just the sad drip of the rain and the darkness.

'Come,' Zalski said. 'Time we are going to the boat.'

'You think you can find it?'

'We are following path. Come.'

Brady wondered how you followed a path through a wood in the dark, but maybe Zalski had cat's eyes. Certainly he showed no sign of hesitation as he led the way in among the trees, and Brady could feel that the ground under his feet was fairly hard and firm in spite of the rain, as though it had been well trodden down under frequent use by walkers. So maybe if they just kept to the harder ground they would not go far wrong even in the dark.

They were walking in single file, Paula just behind Zalski, with Brady bringing up the rear, all keeping close together in order not to lose touch with one another. In one respect the weather was certainly a good ally, since it was unlikely that anyone would be out on such a night for the pleasure of a woodland stroll. And in fact there seemed to be no one about, so maybe if the boat was where it ought to be things might still go well.

Suddenly Zalski came to a halt and they closed up on him. The rain had practically stopped and there was just enough light to reveal that they had come to the edge of the belt of trees. There was an odour of damp earth, and the mournful sound of water dripping from the sodden branches was audible in the stillness.

'Nearly there now,' Zalski said. He was peering ahead, apparently trying to make out some landmark; but it was just one big amorphous shadow, lacking in any kind of definition. Away in the distance on the left some lights glittered through the darkness.

'So where do we go from here?' Brady asked.

He thought Zalski seemed a trifle hesitant now that they had come to the end of the wood. Possibly the directions given by Franz had not been sufficiently precise; and anyway, however precise they might have been, there was the difficulty of seeing anything clearly in such conditions. Nevertheless, Zalski's hesitation was brief.

'Come,' he said. 'This way.'

He began moving forward again, roughly at right angles to the line of trees as far as Brady could tell. But now there was no detectable path underfoot; they seemed to be walking in grass which was long enough to wet the bottoms of Brady's trouser-legs; he could feel the water soaking through to his ankles and chilling his feet. He was glad he had agreed not to bring the suitcase; it would certainly have been a nuisance. Walking through the wet grass had something of the character of a bad dream; there was the same sense of the impossibility of making any appreciable progress and the same indefinable dread of what might be lying in wait.

And then he heard Zalski utter a low exclamation. 'Ah!'

173

Zalski had again halted, and when Brady came up with him and the girl he found that there was a fence in front of them. It was a post and rail fence and only about four feet in height, presenting no great obstacle to their advance.

'Were you expecting this?' he asked.

'Yes,' Zalski said, and he sounded more cheerful. 'Franz is telling me about a fence. Now we are finding it, so is okay, I think.'

'And what next?'

'Next we must be walking that way.' Zalski pointed to the left. 'We must be keeping close to fence until we are finding a ditch in the way.'

He set off at once, following the line of the fence, which was the most tangible guide they had had, and they had walked no more than a hundred yards or so when they came to the ditch. Indeed Zalski was pressing ahead so confidently that he was almost into it before he realised that it was so close. He halted just in time on the very brink. It appeared to be fairly wide and perhaps deep also.

It was obvious that they were not going to get over it, but Zalski said there was no need because this was where they climbed over the fence. On the other side of the fence there was no ditch to contend with; it either ended there or ran under a culvert; it was impossible to tell which in the dark. What there was instead, about ten yards from the fence, was a path and what felt like a tarmac surface. Zalski, with no further hesitation, turned left along the path and a minute or two later again came to a stop.

'There! You see it?'

He was pointing away to the right. Brady could see that there was something, a whitish shape just visible through the gloom. It could have been a shed of some sort.

'What is it?'

'Boathouse,' Zalski said. 'Is river just other side.' He was keeping his voice low, as though he felt the need for extreme caution now.

Brady would have agreed on that point. He peered in the direction of the boathouse and caught a kind of glimmer beyond it. Water! That must be the Oder, the river they had to get past in order to reach Polish soil. His heart-beat quickened.

'Do we just take the boat ourselves?'

'No,' Zalski said. 'There is a man with it. He is to be taking us across.'

'If he's there.'

'He will be there,' the girl said.

Maybe, Brady thought.

His eye was attracted by some lights twinkling through the darkness away to the right. The lights appeared to be moving. He called Zalski's attention to them, but Zalski seemed unconcerned.

'Is barge. Is no need for worrying.'

A moment later Brady caught the faint sound of the diesel engine as the barge dropped down-river towards Frankfurt. Maybe it would stop there for the night.

'Come,' Zalski said.

They advanced cautiously towards the boathouse and halted there while the barge went past. It might have come out of Poland; from Wroclaw perhaps.

'Okay,' Zalski said. 'Let's go.'

There was a small landing-stage and the boat was there. The man was sitting in it, waiting for them. He was in the stern, a dark, hunched figure, his back towards them.

'You see,' the girl murmured softly. 'It is all as arranged.'

Brady said nothing. He could again feel that fluttering sensation in the stomach, the slightly quickened heart-beat. He would not be happy until they were on the other side of the river. And even then not really happy perhaps, since Poland was not England; it was still the devil of a way from home base.

They stepped on to the landing-stage, and they were moving so silently that they failed to rouse the man in the boat. He did not move, did not turn to greet them. They came up from behind him and he was maybe dozing, for he still had not moved when Zalski laid a hand on his shoulder and shook him gently.

He moved then. He fell over sideways and there was a soft thud as his head struck the gunwale of the boat. But even that failed to wake him, and nothing was going to any more.

He was like Henryk Szydiak lying on his blood-soaked bed in the room over the shop in Torun; he was in the long sleep and would never awake again in this world.

Zalski seemed about to try to lift the man up, then saw that it was useless. He let go of the body and at that moment a light was switched on at the end of the landing-stage. He turned quickly, but the other men were already coming out of the boathouse. There must have been half a dozen of them at least, and the odds were hopeless from the start. Zalski was crazy even to try to make a fight of it, but that was the kind of man he was. Brady had not been aware until then that Zalski was carrying a gun, but now he hauled a pistol from some inside pocket and began blazing away before anyone had said a word.

Brady saw the men coming, and then he grabbed the girl and dragged her down flat on the landing-stage just as they started blasting off at Zalski in reply. He heard Zalski give a thin scream and there was a thud as he hit the boards and then no more screaming, so maybe he was dead. The fool, Brady thought, the damned bloody fool! He had got himself killed, and for what? He had never had a hope of shooting his way out of that kind of trouble, but the crazy idiot had had to try it; and now perhaps there would be two more of them with bullets in the heart or the guts or wherever, because those bastards from the boathouse were still shooting and there was not enough cover on the landing-stage to hide a couple of undernourished woodlice.

But suddenly the shooting stopped and he wondered whether he ought to get a handkerchief out of his pocket and wave it as a flag of surrender; but he thought no, if they saw him move they would think he was pulling a gun like that madman Zalski, and they would start blasting again. So he lay there with one arm across the girl's shoulders, holding her down in case she felt any inclination to try a Zalski act herself, and waited for them to come and get him. He was face downward and he could see nothing; his nose and chin were touching the boards, and he could smell the wet timber and it was not the kind of odour he would have walked ten yards to sniff in the ordinary course of things. And then he sensed that somebody was standing over him and looking down, and his flesh crawled a bit, because he could not be sure that the man was not lining up a gun on the back of his head and preparing to squeeze the trigger.

But there was no shot, just a barking laugh and a foot tapping him in the side and playing hell with that spot where Dr Leber had done his little bit of carving and needlework; and he almost let out a yelp of pain but cut it off before it could get out.

Somebody said something which sounded like an order in German, and Paula turned her head and said: 'We're to get up and place our hands on our heads.'

'Let's do it then,' he said; and he took his arm off her shoulders and got up slowly and stood with his hands resting on his head while the girl did the same.

The light on the landing-stage was not terribly brilliant and he could see none of the men very clearly, but he could tell that they were all in uniform except two who were wearing belted raincoats and felt hats. It was one of the felt-hatted who had stood over him and toed him in the side. He got an impression of a blunt sort of face and wide shoulders. He would have liked to give something in return for the pain he had received, but there was really not much chance of that at the moment and he doubted whether there ever would be.

The other felt-hatted man rolled Zalski over with his foot. Zalski made no protest; he lay on his back staring up at the black sky. The second felt-hatted man gave the thumbs-down sign and Brady knew that Zalski was finished. It was a wretched way to go.

He wondered who had betrayed them this time. Franz maybe? But it made no difference. All that mattered was the fact, and the fact was that they were not going back to Poland. Leber and his pals had been right not to trust him with any message or parcel for London; they had been oh so right, so very very right. Damn them.

The man with the blunt face said something and the girl translated it.

'He says we are under arrest.'

'As if we didn't know already,' Brady said.

CHAPTER THIRTEEN

SWILL

His mouth felt as dry as the inside of a limekiln and he guessed that they had been pumping some kind of drug into his system. He was lying on a white iron bed in a small white-painted room which was very much like the one he had occupied after Dr Leber had operated on him. Only this one had a window, which proved that wherever it was, it was not underground.

He had in fact no idea where it was; all he knew was that after the unfortunate affair at the landing-stage he had been bundled into a car and driven away, with the blunt-faced man sitting beside him and two of the uniformed police in the front. It had been a pretty long drive through the night and they had finally arrived at an austere brick building surrounded by a high wall. He had been taken at once to a sparely furnished room where he had been questioned by a large fat man with an ice-bald head and a face like a frog, wide-mouthed, eyes slightly bulging, skin unhealthily mottled and covered with a multitude of warts and other excrescences. This man had introduced himself as Colonel Deutz; he had a voice that fitted well with his appearance, a trifle croaking, but low-pitched and not altogether unfriendly in tone.

'Mr Storey, is it not? Mr Walter Storey.'

'Yes,' Brady said. The passport was lying on the desk in front of Colonel Deutz and the question was no more than a matter of form.

Colonel Deutz gazed at him for a few moments, shaking his head slowly from side to side as though in gentle and regretful admonishment. 'You should not be here, you know. You really have no business to be in the German Democratic Republic at all.'

'I was trying to put that right,' Brady said.

The colonel's left eyebrow rose slightly. 'To put it right?'

'I was about to leave when your people stepped in and prevented me.'

'Ah, yes, but you should never have been here in the first place. Why did you come?'

'I wanted to see what your country was like.'

'And did it come up to your expectations?'

'Completely.'

This was just preliminary sparring of course; they both knew it; they both knew that the real stuff was yet to come. Colonel Deutz seemed to be in no hurry.

Brady was wondering what had happened to the girl. He had not seen her since he had been put into the car and driven away. Had they brought her to this place, too? Was someone else interrogating her in another room? He had no expectation that Deutz would tell him, but he asked nevertheless.

'Do not bother yourself about Miss Nowicki,' Deutz said. 'She is being well taken care of, I can assure you.'

He was not greatly reassured. There were many ways of taking care of people and not all of them were particularly pleasant. He doubted whether Paula would find the care entirely to her liking, but there was nothing he could do to help her; he could not even help himself.

'Now,' Colonel Deutz said; and his voice was just a shade harder, as though the pleasantries had been put aside and it was time to get down to the real business. 'Now suppose you tell me the true reason why you came to the Democratic Republic.'

All that had taken place some time ago. Exactly how long, Brady could not be sure. There was a haziness about the proceedings. He knew that Colonel Deutz had gone on asking questions and he had given evasive answers and it had all seemed to be getting nowhere. But finally Deutz had called in two guards and they had brought him up to this room and made him get into bed. And then a man in a white coat had jabbed a hypodermic syringe into his arm . . .

After that it was really hazy; it was like the blurred recollection of a dream. Deutz came into it, of course; Deutz asking questions, questions, questions, which he answered as well as he could, holding nothing back, doing his best. It seemed to go on and on.

But the interrogation must have come to a conclusion eventually. He had slept. But for how long? He had no idea. It came into his mind that this was not the first time he had been questioned while under the influence of a drug designed to make him reveal the truth. There had been an occasion in Hungary, but then the drug had been experimental and the effects had been quite alarming. This time there was nothing of that kind; merely the dryness in his mouth and a feeling of lassitude.

It was daylight now, that much he could see; but what time of day was it? Instinctively he glanced at his left wrist, but his watch was no longer there. So they had taken that. Well, it was only to be expected. And if they kept it, it would be no great loss; it was only a cheap one and had never been very accurate.

He passed his tongue over his scummy lips and tried to work up some saliva. God, his mouth was dry.

The door opened and Colonel Deutz oozed into the room like some vast fungoid growth that had been equipped with legs. He sank on to a chair by the bed with a hissing sigh.

'And how are you feeling now, Mr Brady?'

'Brady!'

Deutz smiled, the warty face going into all manner of creases. 'Now please don't bother to deny that it is your name. The passport is not yours, of course, and you are not Walter Storey. The real Mr Storey is at present serving a term of imprisonment in one of your country's gaols. Isn't that so?'

'How did you—' Brady began, and stopped.

'How did we obtain that information? Is that what you would like to know? The answer is simple; we got it from you. As you have perhaps already guessed, you have been under the influence of a drug; one of the very latest in this field, I may say, and not yet, I fear, available on the open market. It is really very effective and so much less tedious than the old methods of extracting truth from an unwilling informant; so much quicker and so much less distasteful for all concerned.'

'What did I tell you?'

'Everything. That is to say, you told us everything you know. Unfortunately, there are gaps in your knowledge. It seems your superiors in London did not trust you very fully. That was perhaps wise of them; they probably foresaw the possibility that a situation like this might arise, and they would certainly know that no man can hold out under interrogation indefinitely, even if it is only of the brutal old-fashioned kind. In the end he will talk. Only the man who knows nothing can be trusted to reveal nothing. So they told you only that you were to go to Poland and that someone was to make contact with you. That someone turned out to be a certain Miss Paula

Nowicki—a very charming contact, if I may say so.'

'What have you done with her?' Brady said. 'Damn you! If you've harmed her—'

'What will you do if we have? Anyway, as I told you before, she is being taken care of. If it will ease your mind at all, I can promise you that Miss Nowicki will come to no physical harm.'

'You mean you will simply interrogate her in the same way as you interrogated me?'

'Possibly. Not that she is likely to tell us much, either. She is a foolish young lady but really rather harmless. In a way you and she are much the same—amateurs.' Colonel Deutz spoke with faint contempt; it was as though he resented the necessity of wasting his skill on such unrewarding material. 'And so you travelled to Poland as Walter Storey and were brought into the German Federal Republic hidden in a crate. So ridiculous. You still do not know why you came. To fetch something away? To receive a message? You never did find out. Because of certain unforeseen complications it was decided that you had become a marked man and as a courier were too big a risk. You were therefore told nothing and were sent away empty-handed.'

They had certainly got it all out of him, Brady thought. He hoped they had complete faith in the drug; he would not have been at all happy to hear Deutz announce that they intended trying other methods for corroboration. But Deutz said nothing of the kind; he simply treated his prisoner to a long, thoughtful stare and sighed again. It must have been a great disappointment to him not to be able to extract any more information regarding the true purpose of the assignment. He could not even put his finger on the house to which Brady had been taken, since Brady himself, and presumably Paula also, had only the vaguest idea of its location. Leber and Schmidt were probably assumed names.

'What are you going to do with me?'

'What do you expect us to do with you?' Deutz asked.

'You could send me home.'

He had no real hope that they would. Things never worked out as sweetly as that. But perhaps there was a chance, the faintest sliver of a chance.

Deutz shook his head, banishing this glimmer of hope before it could come to anything. 'That, of course, is impossible, quite impossible.'

'Do you intend to put me on trial?'

'Eventually it may come to that. We shall see. For the present you will be held.'

'Where?'

'In a safe place. You must understand that, amateur or not, you have a certain bargaining value.'

Brady understood that. Even pawns could

be used for barter. Unfortunately, he couldn't imagine anyone in London bothering very much about getting him back. They would probably just cross him off the books.

'So I am not to stay here?'

'Oh, no,' Deutz said. 'We have finished with you. I am sorry to say you may find your next quarters somewhat less comfortable.'

* * *

Deutz had not been exaggerating on that point. No attempt had been made to conceal the fact that the room was nothing more nor less than a prison cell. The furnishing was Spartan in the extreme: a bunk with a hard mattress, some rough grey blankets, a washbasin, a bucket with a lid. There was a steel door with a spyhole; a small barred window admitted no great quantity of light and much of this was absorbed by the gloomy brown paint with which the walls were covered.

He had no knowledge of where he was. He knew only that he had been taken to a car under escort and that the car had travelled for much of the night before finally arriving in the grey light of dawn at this place, which was a big isolated building constructed in the style of a Victorian workhouse. Like the establishment where Deutz had carried out his interrogation, it had a high surrounding wall. Beyond the wall were pine forests.

He was not actively ill-treated. The guards showed no sadistic tendencies, but they spoke no English and communication was minimal. Of other prisoners he saw little; for the greater part of the time he was locked in his cell, and the periods of exercise allowed to him were taken in an enclosed yard where he was accompanied by a guard who usually spent the time leaning against a wall and staring at nothing in particular. Days passed in unrelieved tedium, and the worst part of it was the feeling that he had been completely forgotten, like some paper stowed away in a pigeon-hole for future reference and left to gather dust as the weeks passed, and the months, and the years. Not that he had yet been in the prison for very long; it merely seemed so, and the possibility that he might indeed be left to spend a considerable portion of his life in such a place was a prospect that nearly sent him out of his mind.

He thought of ways of escape. The most hare-brained schemes floated into his head, were examined and rejected. The only time he was out of his cell was when he was taken for exercise, and how could he have eluded the guard? And even if he had managed to do that, how could he have got past the walls? Even outside, where would he have gone? He knew nothing of the country; he did not speak the language; and even the natives themselves found it practically impossible to escape to the

West. There was a wall in Berlin and a line of defences along the western frontier, not to keep people out but to keep them in. So what hope was there for him unless that barter deal which Deutz had vaguely hinted at came to something?

Now and then he felt a little pain in his side. Leber had assured him that it would go away in time, but how much time? Suppose complications had set in. Suppose something was going wrong inside there. Normally he would probably not have given it a second thought, but in the cell he had nothing to take his mind off such questions. He brooded, became morbid. He thought of asking to see a doctor, but decided not to; it was probably nothing and he was not sure he wanted to be pulled about by a prison doctor. Give somebody like that the slightest encouragement and he might start trying a few experiments. He wanted no experiments carried out on his body; he wanted to be in full working order when he got out of there. If he ever did get out.

The weather was turning warmer, the days lengthening. When he went out into the yard for exercise the sun was often very warm and the guard leaning against the wall seemed drowsy; at times he even closed his eyes. The idea of creeping up on him and snatching the pistol from the holster on his belt came into Brady's head. But it was never more than an idea. What would he have done after seizing the pistol? What chance was there of shooting a way out? It was a crazy project.

The prison kitchens backed on to the yard and there was always a row of swill bins standing outside the doorway. Sometimes while Brady was taking his exercise a small. covered truck would drive in through the gateway to the yard and two men would empty the swill into iron drums on the back of the truck. Then they would drive away. The gate was operated by a guard on the outer side, and while the truck was in the yard it was closed. When the swill collectors were ready to leave they would drive up to the gate and give a hoot on the horn and the guard on the other side would open up and let them through. It was a regular routine, and the guard in charge of Brady was obviously so used to it that he took no notice as long as Brady did not approach the truck too closely. The swill collectors scarcely glanced at him; they did the job and went; to them he was just another prisoner, of no especial interest.

It would have been unnatural if Brady had not linked the truck in his mind with his vague plans of escape. After all, the truck passed freely in and out of the prison compound, so why should it not carry him with it? There were, of course, any number of reasons why not. How could he possibly get on the truck without being seen by the guard and the two men? And even if that were possible, how could he conceal himself so as to avoid being spotted by the guard at the yard gate and the other guards at the main gate in the outer wall through which the truck must pass? And again, as always, there came the unanswerable question: even supposing all these obstacles were by some miracle surmounted, how then did he get out of the country?

Forget it, Brady.

Then one day he noticed that there were two different men with the swill truck. One of them was young, fair-haired, stockily built; the other was taller, thinner and older. The older man had lank dark hair and a moustache; he looked as if he had seen a lot of life and not all of it had been good; he had sad, disillusioned eyes. There was nothing sad about the younger man; he had not lived long enough to become disillusioned.

Brady was not particularly interested; he had given up the idea of using the truck as a means of escape; indeed, he was becoming resigned to things as they were. So the swill truck was being operated by two different men. So what of it? Good luck to them. They didn't know how fortunate they were in being able to come and go as they pleased.

It was about a week later when the older man spoke to him. He was standing in the middle of the yard when the truck came in and it passed close to him. The younger man was driving, and as it went past the older man turned his head and spoke just two words: 'Be ready.'

Brady did not move. It was as though for a moment his heart stopped beating and then raced madly ahead. Standing in the hot sun he had a feeling of giddiness, as though the walls of the yard were revolving, the ground shifting under his feet. What did it mean? Be ready! Ready for what?

The truck had come to a halt by the door of the kitchen. The two men were beginning to empty the bins of swill. He glanced towards the guard by the wall. The man had opened his eyes as the truck came in, but now they were closed again; he seemed to be dozing. The stocky young man suddenly detached himself from the truck and ran across the yard as lightly as a ballet dancer. The guard heard him coming at the last moment, but it was too late. The young man had something in his right hand which looked like a short piece of rubber hose. He struck the guard on the side of the head, and the guard's legs bent at the knees and he slid down the wall to a sitting posture with his chin dropping on to his chest. He looked as though he were asleep.

The stocky young man came running back, still with that light, ballet dancer's step. He caught Brady by the arm and propelled him towards the truck.

'Hurry!' he said. 'Hurry!'

The tail-board was down and the older man was standing on the back of the truck under the canvas hood. He reached down and helped Brady up. Brady was moving as if in a dream; it all seemed utterly unreal but he was going along with it. Not that it would go very far; at any moment somebody might step out of the kitchen, look out of a window, see what was going on. But so far nobody had.

'Quick!' the older man said. 'Get inside this.'

It was one of the iron drums; it was empty but it smelt of swill. It was hardly the time to be fussy about a thing like that. Brady climbed into the drum and crouched down. He heard the crash of the tail-board being hooked up, the closing of the cab doors and the starting of the engine. He expected at any moment to hear the sound of an alarm, but there was nothing. The truck began to move.

He knew when it stopped that it was at the first gate. He heard the brief note of the horn and a moment later they were moving on again. He felt sure the guard who operated the gate would glance into the yard and notice that the other guard was sitting on the ground and that the prisoner was gone, but apparently he was an unobservant man and there was still no alarm.

The truck stopped again. They were at the outer gate. Beyond it was freedom and Brady's heart was thumping wildly. The inside of the

194

drum was slimy and he could feel some moisture soaking through his grey prison garb, but it was of no account. He heard someone walk round to the back of the truck, and then he heard a metallic clang as though one of the drums had been struck with an iron rod; then a second and a third. Suddenly the rod struck the drum in which he was hiding and the sound vibrated in his ears. He could not be sure whether the person wielding the rod was counting the drums or testing them for any difference in sound which might indicate that something different from swill was being carried: he could only wait and hope; praying a little, too.

He heard voices; it sounded like an argument. Time was slipping away and every second was precious; very soon the unconscious guard might wake up or someone else might discover that the prisoner had vanished. What were they arguing about? Had the sound made by the drum he was in roused some suspicion that it was not all that it should have been? Would someone climb into the truck and take a look at it?

But there was no sound of the tail-board being lowered, and then the voices stopped and he heard a cab door slam. The truck moved forward again, changed direction and began to gather speed.

CHAPTER FOURTEEN

NIGHT WALK WITH A NUT-CASE

'I think perhaps it's time we introduced ourselves,' the older man said. 'This is Karl.' He indicated the stocky, fair-haired young man who was driving the car.

The car was a Skoda saloon; it had been waiting for them in a rotting wooden shed which looked as though it might once have been used as a stable. Karl had driven the truck into the shed and Brady had climbed thankfully out of the swill drum. The older man was already taking some clothes out of the boot of the Skoda.

'Better change into these. I think they'll fit well enough.'

They had fitted well enough. Brady had asked no questions; there was obvious need for haste and the questions could wait. Within five minutes the change of clothing and vehicles had been made and they were on their way again, Brady riding in the back and the other two in front.

Karl turned his head and grinned at Brady. 'You okay?'

'I'm okay,' Brady said. 'Just bewildered.'

'It's natural,' the older man said. 'I'm Martin.'

'Is that a Christian name or a surname?'

'Christian name. We don't go in for surnames. It's better that way.'

'But I take it you know mine?'

'Yes, we know yours. Both of them. We know quite a lot about you, Mr Brady.'

'You can call me Steve, since we're on first name terms. I think you've earned the privilege anyway.'

'You were tired of being in that place?'

'Who wouldn't be? It's been a long time. I thought everybody had forgotten me.'

'Not quite. But you must understand there were difficulties. In the first place, news of what had happened at the river crossing only leaked through rather slowly. Then we had to find out where they'd taken you, and after that we had to set this thing up. It was done fairly quickly, all things considered.'

'How did you manage it?'

'It was a case of buying the concession from the original swill collector. And of course we had to have forged papers and official approval to carry on the business.'

'But how could you have known it would work? Suppose I hadn't been in the yard.'

'We weren't counting on anything like that; it was by way of a bonus. The most we were hoping for at first was a bit of reconnaissance on the inside. We thought we might work something out from there. But as luck would have it, that wasn't necessary. Sometimes

197

things go like a charm; this happened to be one of those times.'

The man spoke remarkably good English with no trace of a foreign accent.

Brady said: 'You sound as though you were educated in England.'

'Why not?' Martin said. 'Where else would you expect me to be educated?'

'Are you telling me you are English?'

'Precisely.'

'One of the professionals.'

'I'm not sure I get you.'

'It doesn't matter,' Brady said. 'Just a private joke.'

With that lined, angular face of his and those sad, disillusioned eyes, Martin looked like a man who didn't much go in for jokes. Perhaps for the professionals all life was too dead serious.

'And Karl?' Brady said.

'Karl is German.'

Karl grinned again. 'That worry you?'

'Not a bit. I'm not prejudiced.'

The Skoda was travelling pretty fast. Brady wondered just how far they had to go and how long it would be before his escape was discovered and the machine went into action—search, road-blocks, all that kind of thing. They had got on to a good road and there was quite a deal of traffic, but it was not long before Karl took a turning to the right and then they were in the minor road department again.

Brady felt a little safer then: if there were going to be any road-blocks they were likely to be working on the main highways first. Not that any road could be called safe; better to be off them altogether and in some nice secluded sanctuary where they could wait for the hue and cry to die down. If there was such a place. But he supposed Martin and Karl knew what they were doing. He had to hope so, since he was in their hands now.

He said: 'I can't really understand why anyone should have bothered about me.'

Martin turned his head. 'Can't you, old man? Well, I wouldn't know; I'm only carrying out orders. Seems London rather wants to have you back.'

'Frankly,' Brady said, 'I wouldn't have expected London to give a damn. It's been all one big cock-up from start to finish, you know. I'd have said they'd have been only too pleased to write me off.'

'Oh, you mustn't imagine they'd wash their hands of you just because things went wrong. That isn't the way they work.'

'Isn't it?' Brady said. 'I thought it was.'

He was relieved when they got to the end of the journey without being stopped; he had been on edge all the way and it had seemed interminable. In fact, however, little more than half an hour had passed from the time when they had left the prison, and it was quite possible that, unless the guard had recovered from the blow Karl had given him, the escape might even yet be undetected.

The place they arrived at was a small low-roofed cottage on the edge of a straggling village. Karl drove the Skoda round to the back and put it in a rough wooden shed where a lightweight motor-cycle was already standing. They all got out and went into the cottage by the back door which opened straight into the kitchen. Karl led the way through into a sitting-room, very plainly furnished.

'There is a bedroom for you upstairs,' he said. 'You must stay here for the present.'

'For how long?' Brady asked.

'Not long. A day or two perhaps.'

'And then?'

It was Martin who answered this time. 'And then we have to get you out of the country.'

He thought of asking how they proposed doing that, but decided to leave it. If he knew, it might only give him something more to worry about. He had enough worries already, so why add to them?

'Is this place safe?'

Karl gave a wry smile. 'No place is entirely safe.'

'You are as safe here as anywhere,' Martin said. 'There is no reason why anyone should come looking for you here. It would be advisable to stay indoors, not wander round the village.'

'I wasn't thinking of doing that. But suppose they find the swill truck and trace you from that?'

'They won't. That was operated by two entirely different people. Those people have now vanished; they have no connection whatever with us.'

'In this village,' Karl said, 'I am known as a writer. Sometimes I have friends to stay with me. No one is very curious; they regard me as a little eccentric perhaps, that is all. There is a woman who does some work about the house and washes my clothes; she is not talkative; unless you speak directly to her she hardly says a word.'

'Does she understand English?'

'No.'

'Then I won't speak directly to her.'

Karl showed him where he was to sleep. They went up a narrow staircase which twisted acutely and ended at a doorway opening straight into a bedroom. There was a door in the right-hand wall leading to a somewhat smaller room, and in this was a third door which gave access to a tiny chamber wedged into the angle where the roof sloped down to the eaves. There was a dormer window admitting some light and air, but the atmosphere seemed confined and stuffy nevertheless. The chief item of furniture was a camp bed and there was space for little else.

Brady reflected that his cell in the prison had been larger; but for a day or two it would serve. He supposed Karl and Martin had been using the two larger rooms, and there was really no reason why they should move out for him.

Karl looked at him, grinning. 'You think you like this room?'

'I'm not complaining,' Brady said.

'You like to sleep now?'

'No,' Brady said, 'not yet.' He had never felt less inclined to sleep. Maybe Karl thought they had been over-working him at the prison.

'You feel okay?'

'I feel fine.' There was that pain now and then in the side, but it was not worth mentioning. When he got back to England perhaps he would have his own doctor take a look at him. But it could wait.

'Right, then,' Karl said. 'Now I have business to do. I leave you with Martin. Okay?'

'Okay,' Brady said; and he wondered what Karl's business was, but did not ask.

He went down the narrow stairs, leaving Karl in the larger of the two other bedrooms. Martin was in the sitting-room smoking a cigarette. He offered one to Brady.

Brady refused. 'I never touch them.'

'I'm always meaning to give it up,' Martin said, 'but that's as far as it ever gets.'

Brady asked Martin whether he knew what had happened to Paula Nowicki. Martin knew nothing about her; apparently she was not in his brief.

'Maybe they've sent her back home.'

It was possible, Brady thought; but she was not likely to get a heroine's welcome in Poland. He hated to think of her languishing in prison, but what could he do?

Karl came down into the sitting-room. He had changed his clothes and was carrying a white crash-helmet. 'I go now.'

Martin nodded.

Karl went out by the back door and Brady heard the motor-cycle start up. He looked out of the front window and saw Karl ride off in the opposite direction to that from which they had come to the cottage.

'Where is he going?'

'I don't know,' Martin said. It might have been the truth and it might not.

'How long have you been working in East Germany?'

Martin let smoke drift from his mouth. 'I think it would be better if you didn't ask questions.'

'All right,' Brady said. 'But just one more— what do we do to pass the time?'

'We could play cards.'

They played cards. Martin won.

'Will you take an IOU?' Brady asked. 'I haven't got any hard cash.' That seemed to ring some kind of bell. It was the way it had all started; with a gambling debt.

'Forget it,' Martin said. 'Would you like to eat?'

'It sounds a good idea.'

They had a meal in the kitchen. There was a larder stocked with food, an oil-stove for cooking. There was no main water, just a pump over a stone sink; no electricity.

'The primitive way of life,' Martin said.

'It's better than prison.'

*　　　*　　　*

It was evening when Karl came back. They were playing cards again and they heard the sound of the motor-cycle. Karl came in through the kitchen, the white crash-helmet in his hand.

'Any trouble?' Martin asked.

'No trouble. They've been checking cars and trucks. They checked me, but they weren't very interested. I wasn't carrying anyone on the pillion.'

'So what now?' Brady asked.

Karl grinned. 'Now we eat.'

When it grew dark Karl lit an oil-lamp and drew the curtains. As if it had been a hint Martin got up from his chair and went upstairs. Brady could hear him moving about overhead and he looked at Karl.

'Does he usually go to bed as early as this?'

'He has not gone to bed,' Karl said. 'He is preparing to send a signal.'

'Signal?'

'Radio.'

'Oh,' Brady said, 'so there's a transmitter up there?'

Karl nodded.

Brady hoped Martin knew what he was doing. If he went on too long the transmission might be picked up and located by East German monitors. But of course he knew that; he was a professional; he had had experience.

A little later Martin came downstairs again.

'Okay?' Karl asked.

'It's okay,' Martin said. 'Tomorrow. They'll be waiting.'

'What happens tomorrow?' Brady asked.

He half expected Martin to tell him again not to ask questions, but this time he got an answer.

'Tomorrow you go over into West Germany.'

He was not sure it was quite the answer he would have liked. What precisely did Martin mean by that bald statement? It needed a bit of amplification, because they all knew that going over into West Germany was not quite as simple as it sounded; it was not a question of merely taking a stroll down the road; there was a lot more to it than that, a hell of a lot.

'Now just how,' he said, 'are you proposing I should do that?'

'By crossing the border, of course. Karl will go with you.

Karl nodded. 'Tomorrow night.'

'Now wait,' Brady said. 'I may not be very bright, but to me it seems there's one little snag.'

'Yes?' Martin waited for him to go on.

'Like a lot of defensive garbage along the frontier designed to prevent people doing just what you're proposing Karl and I should do. Have you thought about that?'

'Naturally we've thought about it. These things are not done on the spur of the moment. Tell him, Karl.'

Karl found a sheet of paper and a pencil and began to make a sketch, sitting at the table with the light from the oil-lamp picking out glints of gold in his hair. Brady looked at the sketch and his blood began to pick up a distinct chill even before Karl started explaining what the pencil marks represented. When he did start explaining Brady wanted to run away and dig a hole in the ground. It was crazy; it was sheer bloody suicide; nobody but a madman would even think of trying it.

'The first tripwires,' Karl said, 'are about five kilometres from the border. They set off alarms in hidden police pill-boxes.'

'Well, that finishes it for a start. No need to go any further. The police come out and catch us. Curtains.'

Karl shook his head. 'We do not trip on the wires.'

'All right, so we manage to get past them.

206

What's the next hazard?'

'Dogs. They are on long leads which slide along other wires. But they are no problem.'

'No?'

'No. So now we are past the dogs and we come to a deep trench with steep sides. That is easy.'

'If you say so. What next?'

'A fine-mesh steel fence four metres high. On top of the fence is a knife-edge sharp enough to cut the hands to pieces. After that a minefield, then the barbed-wire.'

Brady had stopped asking questions. He just felt sick.

'On the other side of the barbed-wire entanglement,' Karl said, 'is another steel fence. It is not quite as simple as the first one because there are splinter bombs with cone-shaped projectors fixed to the concrete posts at three different heights. If you trigger off these devices they throw out a hail of jagged metal in a fan which can tear you to shreds. When you are over that fence there is a strip of open ground which is floodlit and can be raked with fire from observation posts. Beyond that is the border. Where we will cross there is a belt of trees on the West German side. When we have made it to the trees we are home and dry.'

Karl put down his pencil and sat back with the satisfied air of a man who had successfully completed a difficult crossword puzzle. Brady remained perfectly still and could feel the ice collecting round his heart. Martin took out a cigarette and lit it over the chimney of the lamp.

Karl said: 'You don't say nothing.'

Brady found his voice, though he hardly recognised it; it had a sound like a squeaky hinge. 'You're crazy. There isn't a hope.'

'It's the only hope there is,' Martin said. 'You'll never get out any other way.'

'I'll never get out this way. I'll just end up being eaten by dogs or blown to bits or shot in the head. It can't be done. You know it can't.'

'It's been done,' Karl said. 'I have done it.'

Brady stared at him in disbelief. 'You!'

'I went across with another man.'

'And came back the same way?'

'No. There are other ways of getting back.'

'But I don't see how it's possible. I just don't see how.'

'There are weaknesses in every system.'

'But the minefield and the barbed-wire.'

'There are ways through; there have to be. There are times when it is necessary for the border guards to pass from one side to the other.'

'And you know these ways?'

'Not all, of course. But we need only one.'

'But what about the splinter bombs on the last fence?'

'Where we go they will not be working.'

'How do you know that?'

'Men can be bought even in a Communist country.'

So someone had been bribed; perhaps more than one. But could they depend on it?

'And the floodlights?'

'They will not be working, either.'

The ice round Brady's heart had melted slightly; not much, but a little. Karl picked up the sketch and held it over the chimney of the lamp until the paper caught fire. He carried it by one corner to the fireplace and let it burn away to ashes in the hearth. For a while he stood looking thoughtfully down at the charred bits of paper; then turned.

'This time,' he said, 'I think maybe I don't come back.'

Brady saw how it was: the game was getting a little too hot for him. He had decided to call it a day and come in from the heat.

*   *   *

Brady had about as wretched a night's sleep as he could remember. And it was not the cramped quarters or the camp bed that were the cause; he could have taken them in his stride after weeks in a prison cell. But the thought of what was on the programme for the next night kept him wakeful for much of the time and plagued with nightmares for the rest of it. He rose in the morning feeling a haggard wreck and had very little appetite for breakfast.

Martin looked at him with some concern. 'Are you feeling all right?'

'I've felt better,' Brady said. 'I slept badly.'

'You're not worried, are you?'

'Are you kidding? I'm worried sick. A man would need to be round the bend not to be worried with this thing hanging over him.'

'Karl isn't worried.'

Which, Brady thought, proved nothing except maybe that Karl was round the bend. It was a pleasant thought. So he had a nut-case to take him past all those damned obstacles the East Germans had set up to make sure their happy citizens didn't manage to escape from the Communist Utopia. Night walk with a nut-case. Nice prospect.

'I'm still not sure I'll go.'

'Of course you'll go,' Martin said. 'What alternative have you got?'

'I could stay here.'

'For how long?'

Brady could see it was not a feasible alternative. If he refused to go there was only one thing he could do: give himself up and go back to prison.

'Do you think we went to all the trouble of springing you just to have you chicken out when it came to the crunch?' Martin said. 'Did you expect it to be a cake-walk all the way?'

'I didn't expect to have to walk through minefields and barbed-wire.'

'It's all in the day's work.'

'Not where I come from.'

'Well, the sooner you do it, the sooner you'll be back where you come from.'

There was something in that, Brady thought.

'You'll do it,' Martin said.

And he probably would—when it came to the crunch.

*   *   *

The woman arrived later to sweep up and wash the dishes and make the beds. She brought some clean washing and she looked at Brady but said nothing; she seemed unsurprised to see him. She was about fifty; fat, with a waddling gait and dropsical ankles. Brady looked back at her and decided she didn't look like a spy or an informer. Maybe if she had found the two-way radio she would not have known what it was; but presumably Martin kept it well hidden when it was not in use. She cleared off after about an hour and it was dead quiet. Karl had gone off somewhere in the Skoda and Martin was reading a book. It was a hot day and Brady dozed in an armchair, making up for some of his lost sleep.

Karl returned late in the afternoon. He came in lugging a canvas kit-bag, which he dumped on the floor of the kitchen.

'Any road-blocks?' Martin asked.

Karl shook his head. 'Things seem to have cooled off.'

'They'll still be looking, though.'

'Oh, sure; they'll still be looking.'

Brady hoped they would not look too closely. But at least if they found him in time he would be spared that spine-chilling assault course to the border. He was not absolutely sure whether he wanted to be found or not.

They had a meal. Karl said it was best to give the food time to be digested before they started. He ate heartily, so it looked as though his nerves were not troubling him; but Brady was so tensed up he had difficulty in forcing anything down.

Martin noticed. 'You'll be all right when you get going,' he said. 'It's thinking about it that's the worst part.'

'I hope you're right,' Brady said, 'but I'm not counting on it.'

It was about ten o'clock when Karl stood up and said it was time to be getting ready. Brady thought of suggesting that they should wait until the next night, anything to postpone this crazy business; but he knew the other two would never agree to that; it had been set up for this night, and this night it would have to be.

Karl fetched the kit-bag and started taking things out of it. There was quite a variety of articles: a length of nylon rope to which was attached a grapnel, an iron stake with triangular flanges on each side, a mallet with a padded head, some objects made of light metal which looked rather like angle-irons with a hook at one end, an air-pistol, two black climber's helmets, a flat round tin, two bullet-proof waistcoats, a strip of what appeared to be chain-mail and a small rucksack.

Karl handed one of the bullet-proof waistcoats to Brady and told him to put it on.

'So you're expecting to get shot at?' Brady said.

'It is best to be prepared.'

Brady put the waistcoat on over his shirt, and a windcheater over the waistcoat. He was sweating slightly and felt a certain constriction of the chest. Karl had put on the other waistcoat and was stowing the rest of the gear in the rucksack; all except the climber's helmets, one of which he passed to Brady.

'You may as well wear that.'

Brady put the helmet on and fixed the strap under his chin. He had a sense of inevitability now; there was no longer any possibility that the whole thing would fade away like a bad dream; it had started and it would go on.

'We shall be riding the motor-cycle,' Karl said. 'It will be best if you carry the rucksack for the present. Later I will take it. Okay?'

'Okay,' Brady said. He shrugged himself into the shoulder-straps of the rucksack. There was a faint rattle of metal but the weight was not excessive.

Karl had put on the second helmet. 'So. We are ready?'

'Ready,' Brady said; and he felt like death.

Martin came out with them to the shed. It was a still, clear night, not moonlit but with a starry summer radiance that was far from utter darkness. Karl wheeled out the motor-cycle and straddled it. Brady got on behind him.

'Good luck,' Martin said.

Brady wondered what Martin proposed to do. Take the Skoda and vanish? Maybe. But that was his affair.

Karl kicked the engine into life. It made surprisingly little noise.

Here we go, Brady thought; here we go and we're both mad, mad as they come.

CHAPTER FIFTEEN

OBSTACLE COURSE

Karl opened the tin. 'Take some.'

'What is it?' Brady asked.

'Blacking. For the face and hands. So we aren't seen so easily.'

Brady dipped his fingers into the tin and began to smear his face. It was all very quiet now that the engine of the motor-cycle had stopped. They were off the road and in among some bushes; from there, Karl had said, they would have to go on foot; it would be about three kilometres before they came to the fringe of the border defences. He saw Karl take the air-pistol out of the rucksack, break it open and slip something into the breech. A pellet presumably. But what good would an air-pistol be? You couldn't stop a man with that. Karl stuck the pistol in his belt and hoisted the rucksack on to his shoulders.

'Ready?'

'Ready,' Brady said.

At first there was a footpath. Later they left the path and struck out across open ground; heathland, uneven; clumps of trees looming here and there like grotesque, shadowy monsters; now and then a rabbit scampering away; an owl hooting. Karl was in the lead,

Brady following close at his heels, wondering how he could find the way, how he could be sure he was on the right track.

They travelled at a brisk pace for the first part of the way, but then Karl slowed down and seemed to be going more warily. Suddenly he came to a halt. Brady stopped also. Karl was bending down, apparently peering at the ground.

'What is it?' Voice kept low.

'A tripwire,' Karl said.

He pointed at it with his finger. When Brady stooped he could see it a little way above the ground. Karl must have had uncanny perception to have detected it. They stepped over it carefully and went on. There were more wires to negotiate, spaced out at varying distances. Karl found them all.

They came to a gully and rested there. Brady was beginning to have more respect for Karl's abilities; but they had as yet merely touched on the problem; the real test was still to come.

He heard, a faint sound and felt the touch of Karl's hand on his arm. He heard the low whisper of Karl's voice and detected the urgency in it.

'Look!'

He turned his head and looked. A man was standing on the lip of the gully, silhouetted against the night sky. He had what appeared to be a submachine-gun under his arm;

impossible to tell whether he was looking down into the gully or not. For perhaps half a minute he stood perfectly still while they lay watching him, motionless also; then he seemed to fumble in his pocket and a moment later a match spurted into flame and the scent of cigarette smoke drifted down to them.

'Wait here,' Karl whispered.

He moved noiselessly away, keeping close to the ground. In a moment Brady had lost sight of him in the shallow gully.

He waited. The man with the gun was placidly smoking his cigarette; now and then the glow of the tip was visible as he drew smoke into his mouth. Karl rose suddenly from the ground behind him; for a moment the two figures merged into one; there was a grunting sound, then the cigarette shed sparks as it fell and the man dropped forward on top of it. Karl came back down the gully with cat-like steps and wiped the blade of his knife on the grass.

'You've killed him,' Brady said. It had been done so swiftly, so noiselessly, that it was difficult to believe. He had not even known that Karl was carrying a knife.

'It was necessary.'

'He hadn't seen us.'

'We could not be sure he would not.'

'So you made sure?'

'Yes.' Karl slid the knife back into the sheath on his belt. 'Come. There is no time

217

to lose.'

He picked up the rucksack and they went on. The dead man lay where he had fallen. Brady wondered how long it would be before his absence was noticed. They certainly had no time to lose now.

*   *   *

It was a sound like that of a curtain-ring sliding along a brass rod, very faint; that and a soft padding of paws, nothing more; the dog itself was silent. It was already leaping at him when Brady turned to face it, launching itself from the ground like a canine projectile. He jerked back and heard the vicious snap of jaws as the dog missed his throat by inches. The shoulder of the brute struck him on the chest; he was already off balance and he fell over backwards. The dog turned quickly and came at him again. He brought his feet up as he lay on his back and kicked it in the belly. It gave a low howl of pain, rolled over and was in again quickly. He felt the teeth sink into his left shoulder and he was thankful for the bullet-proof waistcoat; even a Doberman pinscher's jaws were not strong enough to bite through that. He tried to push the dog off, but it held on, and he was afraid it might let go of his shoulder and make another snap at his throat; and he remembered that Karl had said the dogs were no problem. No problem? Like hell, they weren't! And where was Karl, anyway? Why wasn't the bastard in there helping? This was surely the time when he could have used some help, because he was damned soon going to have his throat ripped out if something was not done about it.

And then he heard the sound of the air-pistol very close, like a kind of dry gasp, and the dog let go of his shoulder and seemed to shudder a little and lie still. He got to his feet and saw Karl with the gun in his hand. He was surprised that one small pellet from an air-pistol could kill a dog so easily. He told Karl so, and Karl laughed softly.

'It was a dart. The dog is not dead; it is just drugged. Later it will wake up, but we will not be here. Come.'

* * *

'You cannot see them,' Karl said, 'but there are spikes at the bottom. Fall on them and you die very slowly, very painfully. Better not to fall.'

He had said nothing about spikes until then; he had just said there was a deep trench; no mention of anything in it. Brady looked down into the darkness and could see nothing, not even the bottom. The sides of the trench were sheer; no hope of climbing out if you fell in— quite apart from the spikes.

Karl eased the rucksack from his shoulders

and groped about inside it until he found the flanged iron stake and the padded mallet. He stepped six paces back from the edge of the trench and drove the stake firmly into the ground, the impact of the mallet making very little sound because of the muffling effect of the thick padding. He took the nylon rope from the rucksack and tossed the grapnel across to the other side of the trench. He hauled in the rope until the grapnel caught. He put his full weight on it, but the grapnel held firm.

'Good,' he muttered.

There was an eye in the top of the flanged stake. He passed the rope through the eye, drew it taut and fastened it. He closed the rucksack and hoisted it on to his shoulders.

'I will go first,' he said. 'You follow.'

He went across quickly, hanging under the rope like a sloth on a branch. The rope sagged and he had a little difficulty on the far side, but he made it. Brady could just see him standing there, waiting.

Brady thought of the spikes at the bottom of the trench but no amount of thinking was going to make them melt away, so he had better be on his way. He lay down at the edge and reached out to get a grip on the rope with his hands and began to drag himself out over the trench. He hooked his ankles over the rope as Karl had done, hung underneath it and pulled himself along hand over hand. He was about half-way across when he felt the rope give, and he knew that it must be either the stake or the grapnel coming out. Maybe Karl had loosened one or the other when he had gone across and a second load was just one too many.

He stopped moving and hung there on the sagging rope, and it gave a little more and he thought again of the spikes that would drive into his back if he dropped. He heard Karl calling to him, not loudly but urgently.

'Come! Come quickly now! Don't wait!'

There was nothing else he could do; he got moving again, and because of the increased sag of the rope it was uphill work. He could feel the sweat running from him and it was not helping the grip of his hands; but he was nearly there. Another foot or two . . .

It was the stake that failed him. It came out suddenly and he was falling. But he still clung to the rope with hands and feet, and the grapnel was holding, so that he swung like the bob of a pendulum and hit the side of the trench but not the bottom.

He hung there, not even trying to climb; too exhausted to do anything but hang on. A little longer and he knew he would not be able to do even that; he would fall into the trench, fall on to the spikes . . .

It took him a few seconds to figure out what it was that had taken a grip on his collar, to figure out that Karl was leaning over the edge of the trench and had managed to reach him with one hand. He heard Karl's voice in his ear, a trifle hoarse but still urgent.

'Now! Climb, Steve, climb! You can do it!'

And he found he could do it. With Karl's help he was climbing; he was on the lip of the trench; he had his chest over the edge; Karl had got him with both hands; he was out.

He lay for a while letting the sweat cool, letting the trembling go out of his limbs. But not for long. Karl was eager to go, and Brady himself could see that it was no place in which to take one's ease. He stood up and they went forward again; again with Karl in the lead.

When they came to the fence it was easy to see that it was not the kind you could climb without help of some sort. Or if you could not see it, you could feel it: the mesh was too small to allow the fingers to be pushed through and there was no way of getting a grip on it; it was strictly for the cats. The fact that there was a knife-edge along the top was of rather academic interest if there was no way of reaching as high as that.

'Well?' Brady said. 'What do we do about this?'

Karl did not bother to answer; he already had the ruck-sack on the ground and was taking out some of the metal objects which Brady had thought looked like angle-irons with hooks on them. He realised now what their purpose was: hooked on to the steel mesh of the fence they formed projecting steps or handholds. There were some left over, and these Karl stuffed into his pockets.

'For the last fence,' he explained.

He took out the roll of chain-mail and threw the rucksack away; it had served its purpose and there was no point in carrying it any further. He began to climb the fence with the help of the metal steps hooked onto it, and when he had reached the top he unrolled the strip of chain-mail and hung it over the cutting edge. Thus protected from the blade, he climbed over to the other side, hung for a moment by his hands and dropped softly to the ground.

Brady followed quickly. With the steps hooked to the fence and the chain-mail rendering the knife-edge harmless, it was easy. In a moment he had joined Karl.

'Now,' Karl said, 'we must go very carefully. We have to go through the minefield and a step in the wrong place would be rather unfortunate.'

It was hardly an overstatement, Brady thought.

Karl began to walk. Brady tried to step in his exact footmarks; as long as Karl had passed safely it was pretty certain that there were no mines in that particular piece of soil. But maybe they had not yet come to the minefield.

A few minutes later Karl halted. He appeared to be peering into the gloom ahead, and for the first time he seemed to be a trifle uncertain.

'What's wrong?' Brady asked.

'I am looking for a small hill,' Karl said. 'It should be somewhere near here, but I do not see it. Well, we must go a bit further.'

He began to walk again, moving a shade more to the left. Brady followed, not at all happy about it. If Karl had lost his bearings what was to prevent them from stumbling on to a whole nest of mines? But a minute or two later Karl stopped again and Brady saw that he was pointing.

'There! Do you see it?'

Brady looked in the direction indicated and could just discern the outline of a low mound shaped like a barrow and scarcely meriting the name of hill. Growing on the ridge were four trees.

'Now I know where I am,' Karl said.

Brady was glad to hear it. All he knew was that they were in a hell of a situation, and maybe the worst was still to come. But Karl was moving on again and there was nothing for it but to follow.

They came to the mound and skirted the base of it and came to the stake. The stake was about three feet high and was painted white; it showed up quite clearly in the starlight.

'This is the first marker,' Karl said. 'We must keep to the right of it. And now we must be very careful indeed. Come.'

It would, Brady supposed, have been simple enough to follow the markers in daylight, since they were not very far apart. Unfortunately, they were far enough to make it impossible even with the stars brightly shining to pick up the next stake while standing beside the preceding one. It was necessary, therefore, to step out in the supposedly correct direction and keep moving hopefully forward until a glimmer of white came into view. Midway between the stakes neither of them could be seen, and whichever way you stepped you could be in trouble. Brady was sweating again. He guessed Karl was, too, if the truth were told. They should have brought a torch; but he supposed if you started flashing a torch around there you might as well give up anyway.

Karl had stopped again. There was no sign of any marker anywhere; neither in front nor behind; neither to the left nor to the right.

'I have counted eight,' he said. 'There should be ten altogether. We ought to be seeing the ninth by this.'

'You think we've gone off the track?'

'Either that or the stake has been removed.'

'Why would anyone do that?'

'I don't know.'

'Well, we can't just stay here.'

'No; we must go on. Time is slipping away.'

Brady would not have argued about that. There was no telling how soon the dead man might be discovered, and when that happened the balloon would surely go up. But still Karl made no move. Could it be that he was losing his nerve? If so they were really in trouble. Yet who could blame a man for hesitating when his next step might set off a mine and blow him to bits?

Nevertheless, he did move at last. He gave a kind of low sigh and took one cautious step and then another. Brady stayed close behind. A few minutes later they saw the ninth stake. It was away to the right and it should have been on the left.

Again they halted.

'We are off line,' Karl said.

What he did not say, but what both of them knew, was that there must now be mines between them and the safe path. If they went back the chances were that they would step on one; it was only luck that had saved them so far.

Karl sighed again. 'It must be done.' He took the knife from its sheath and carefully prodded the ground in front of him. He took a step forward and prodded again. He had moved two yards towards the stake in this fashion when Brady heard the hiss of his breath being sharply drawn in.

'I have found something.'

'A mine?'

'Perhaps.'

He withdrew the knife with great care and prodded the ground to his left. Again that hissing intake of breath.

'Another.'

He tried to the right. Tried again. Found nothing.

'This way. But carefully.'

Brady needed no such admonition; he set his feet down as lightly as if they had been made of fragile glass. Karl shifted a little to the right, then went forward again, still testing the ground with that delicate probing of the knife.

It took ten more minutes to reach the stake, and Brady felt like a used dishcloth. They picked up the last marker with no difficulty at all.

'And now,' Karl said, 'the barbed-wire.'

There was nothing so nerve-racking about the wire; it was simply a question of finding the place where the opening was situated. It was not easy to see and they walked past it twice before Karl spotted where one of the coils of wire was hooked on to a post. He unhooked it and pushed it to one side. From there a zigzag path led through the entanglement and came out on the other side.

'There is now just the last fence,' Karl said. 'Very soon we are home and dry.'

Brady detected a note of exultation in his voice. He hoped Karl would not be over-confident now in some kind of reaction to that moment in the minefield when he had briefly lost his nerve. This was no time to become reckless; they were not quite home and dry yet;

there was still the last fence. They began to walk towards it.

There was a dip in the ground and pale wraiths of mist floated round them, cold and clammy. Brady shivered, the sweat again cooling on him. His heart was beating fast. It was near now, so very near. Just a little further.

They came out of the hollow, out of the mist, and saw the last fence. There was no floodlighting visible on the other side, so it looked as though the bribery had worked. Good for Karl! He really did know his job. Maybe he was not such a nut-case after all.

They walked up to the fence. Brady could see the cones fixed to the concrete post, but it was all right; they would not be working. He watched Karl take the metal steps from his pockets and hook them on to the mesh, one above another. He put his foot on the lowest one and started to pull himself up, and that was when it happened; that was when it all went wrong.

Somebody had cheated. Somebody had taken the money and not done the job. Maybe Karl should never have tried it a second time; maybe he should have thought himself lucky to get away with it once; it had been crazy to try again. He would not be going back. Well, that was true; unless they shovelled up the pieces and carried him back in a box.

He had been close to the post when he started to climb and he had taken the full blast. It was that which had saved Brady. Brady was flung down, and something slammed into his chest like a hammer but failed to penetrate the bullet-proof waistcoat. Something else, something warm and slimy, fell from the helmet and slid down his cheek. He put a hand to his face and flung the mess away in disgust, with a gesture of revulsion.

His ears were still ringing from the explosion of the splinter bombs, but his mind was working. He was thinking: I'm all right. I haven't been injured. I can climb the fence and there won't be any more bombs to go off until somebody comes and replaces them. So I'd better go now while the going's good. It's no use thinking about Karl; I can't do anything for the poor sod now; nobody can; he's finished. So come on, Brady; get weaving; get the hell out of it.

He stood up and he was feeling groggy, but he got to the fence, and the steps were still there hanging on the mesh, and he went up and crawled over the top. There was no knife-edge on this one, just a strand or two of barbed-wire and he didn't give a damn about that even if it did tear his hands. He hung for a moment and let himself drop; and he fell over when he hit the ground, but he was up in a moment and starting to run. He could see the belt of trees ahead, just the way Karl had said, and he knew that he had only to get across this strip of bare ground and he would be there. It was the last lap and he was going to make it; nothing could stop him now.

He was just about half-way to the trees when the floodlights came on. So they were cheating on that, too; somebody was doing a real double-cross and no mistake. The lights had him and he knew what it felt like to be a rabbit caught in the beam of a car's headlamps. For a moment, like the rabbit, he froze; but then the machine-guns opened up and he got going again, running, crouched low, not zigzagging but just going straight for the trees.

Something gave him a thump in the back and he went over in a somersault, but the bullet-proof waistcoat had done its work and he was on his feet again and plunging ahead in a lunging, lurching run like a drunk in a hurry. His legs were bending and his heart pumping, but he was in the trees; he had made it; he was across the border; he was home and dry.

He was lying on the ground then, lying on his back and staring up at all those shadowy figures gathered round him. There were men in uniform, men in plain clothes, and there was somebody else. And he really had to be dreaming now, because it looked like Linda Manning, and that was crazy. But then she was kneeling down beside him, and she had an arm round his shoulder and was kissing him, and never mind the blood on his face; never mind anything.

And 'Oh, Steve, Steve!' she was saying. 'Oh, Steve darling, you do get yourself into trouble, don't you?'

He thought that was pretty rich coming from her, because whose idea had it been in the first place, for Pete's sake? But he said nothing; he was too damned tired. All he wanted was to have a bath and crawl into the sack; and if she liked to crawl in with him that was all right, too; just as long as she kept very very quiet . . .

CHAPTER SIXTEEN

PAPER AND STRING

It was almost the end of summer when he came out of hospital. It was a very select hospital, very select indeed. He had had a private room and it must have cost a packet. Not that he was worried about that; somebody else would pay.

He had told them there was nothing wrong with him, but it had been no use. He had been flown back from Germany in an R.A.F. transport plane with Linda Manning for company, and they had rushed straight to the hospital in an ambulance; it had been the V.I.P. treatment all along the line. Then they had given him a thorough examination and told him they would have to operate. He seemed to have heard that one before and he told them so. But they were very persuasive, and before the day was out they had him laid out on the table and when he came round it had been done.

There was one thing about it: he would not have another scar, because they had cut him in the same place where Dr Leber had had his little nibble. And there was another thing, too: it was a real solid job this time. Now that it had healed up he could feel nothing of it; none of those twinges of pain he had had before. So maybe Dr Leber had not been so hot after all.

He had been back in the old pad just a day when Linda Manning called to see him. She had visited him a few times at the hospital while he was convalescing, and he was glad to see her any time, except when there was some job she was forcing him to take.

'Well, now,' he said, 'isn't this nice!' And he ushered her in and shut the door and invited her to sit down on one of the clapped-out armchairs with the uncut moquette and the broken springs. 'That's if it's a social visit and not business.'

'It's a little of both,' she said.

'I can't work,' Brady said quickly. 'I'm on the sick list.'

She gave him a critical inspection. 'You don't look at all sick to me. I'd say you were in rude health.'

'Maybe I am, but I'm not working. Not yet.'

'You don't have to. I've brought your pay. That's the business.'

Brady stared at her. 'They're going to pay me? On top of settling the gambling debt.'

'Why, certainly.'

'How much?'

'Four thousand, five hundred and fifty pounds.'

'Now I know you're kidding.'

'No kidding, Steve. It's to make up the round five thousand, which Turner thinks is a reasonable fee.' She opened her handbag and hauled out a wad of notes. It was a nice thick wad and they appeared to be mostly twenties, which was a value Brady didn't handle much in the ordinary way; though he had no objection to doing so. 'Why don't you count it?'

He took the wad from her and flipped it with his thumb. 'There's four thousand, five hundred and fifty here?'

'Yes.'

'I'll take your word for it. But why?'

'You did a job of work. Turner is very pleased. Everybody is.'

'But it was a flop. It all went wrong.'

'Not entirely.'

'Well, I don't see where it went right. I went to Poland; I was taken to East Germany; I was brought out of East Germany; and that's all. I didn't bring any message; I didn't bring anything. They decided they couldn't risk it. I told you all about that.'

'Of course you did. But you did bring something back. You didn't know it but you brought back just what you were sent there for.'

'Oh? And what was that?'

'A little piece of metal. A new kind of toughened steel which is to be used in the latest Soviet tanks and which has been developed in a research establishment at Frankfurt-an-der-Oder.'

Bells were beginning to ring, loud and clear.

'The metal man!'

'Metal man?'

'Schmidt. Zalski said he was a metal man. He meant a metallurgist. So he was the one who pinched the sample?'

'Yes.'

'Why did he do it?'

'The oldest of reasons. Money. Just money.'

'What will he do with the money? He can never spend it on riotous living. Not in East Germany.'

'Oh, he's not having any of it. He's got a daughter living in the States; we are to pay her. Maybe she'll throw it away on a Rolls-Royce and a mink coat, and maybe he'll be shot in a cellar.'

'If they find out what he did.'

'Oh, they will. Sooner or later they will.'

Brady thought she was probably right about that. Schmidt had looked a born loser.

'But I still don't understand how I brought it back. They didn't give me anything.'

She was smiling at him. 'Are you sure about that?'

And then he got it; he must have been slow not to think of it before. It was so obvious now. 'Dr Leber. That operation. There was nothing wrong with me. He was putting that bit of metal in my flesh. And then when I went into hospital back here they took it out again.'

'I'm sure you feel much better without it.'

'So I was just the wrapping for the parcel. A

bit of paper and string.'

'You could put it that way,' she said. 'And there was a message too, of course.'

'A message?'

'A formula, to be more precise. It's amazing the amount that can be engraved on a tiny piece of toughened steel by modern techniques. Now you see why Turner is so pleased. He thinks you did an excellent job, in the circumstances.'

'But he doesn't want me to go and see him?'

'He thought you'd rather see me.'

'He was right about that.' Brady put the wad of notes on the table. 'Would you care for a cup of tea?'

'Thank you,' she said. 'I'm dying for one.'

He went to the kitchenette and put the kettle on, took down the tea-caddy, rinsed out the two cups that were not cracked, found half a bottle of milk and a bag of sugar.

'Incidentally,' Linda said, 'you may be interested to hear that we've had news of a dear friend of yours.'

Brady poked his head out of the kitchenette. 'Who?'

'Paula Nowicki.'

He came completely out. 'You have?' He had been trying to find out what had happened to her ever since his return to London, but nobody seemed to know a thing. 'Where is she?'

'According to our information she's back at

that theatre, cabaret, or whatever it is, where you first contacted her.'

'The Zoppotski?'

'That's the place.'

'So they didn't sling her in gaol. I wonder why.'

'Well, apparently she's very popular. Perhaps they decided the best thing was to give her a caution and make sure she behaves herself in future.'

'I'm glad,' Brady said. 'I was worried about her. It seems as though the Polish authorities really are softening up.'

'There is of course, another possible explanation.'

'Which is?'

'That she was working for the other side.'

Brady was startled. 'Working for them! But she was working for you.'

'It's been done.'

'Are you saying she's a double-agent?'

'I'm saying it's a possibility. She had every opportunity.'

'But that's nonsense.'

'Not at all. She could have arranged for Szydiak to be killed, counting on the probability that she would then be given the job of taking you on to the next contact.'

'No,' Brady said. 'She was really sick when she saw Szydiak lying dead in his room. There was no counterfeit about that.'

'That proves nothing. Besides, she may have

thought they would simply get him out of the way. And maybe that's all they would have done if he hadn't put up a fight. And when she got to Leszno it was easy enough to persuade Zalski to take her on to the end of the journey, which would of course have been her object. It was probably she who alerted the border guards, not Malkowicz, as you imagined.'

'No, she couldn't have done that. She was with me all the time.'

She gave him a keen look. 'All the time?'

He suddenly remembered that early morning walk Paula had taken in Leszno and it stopped him in his tracks. She had said it was to get a breath of fresh air, but could it not just as well have been to find a telephone? He began to have doubts.

'Well, anyway,' he said, 'why did the East German lot try to stop us if what they wanted was to find out where we were going?'

'But they didn't try to stop you. They were only tailing you until Zalski decided to take action. That's what you told me.'

He had to admit that that was true, but he refused to give up. 'You've still got to explain why Paula didn't reveal the situation of that place near Frankfurt-an-der-Oder and have the police raid it.'

'But you said yourself she wasn't allowed out of the basement of the house any more than you were.'

'All right, but it still doesn't fit. If she was on

238

their side she'd have told them about that bit of metal inside me, and they'd have cut me open as soon as they got their hands on me.'

'Oh, no. She didn't know about that, either.'

He was getting checked on every move. 'Well, she couldn't have arranged the ambush at the river. She had no chance.'

Linda admitted this point. 'No; that must have been someone else. Someone involved in setting up the plan to get you across perhaps.'

'My bet is Franz.'

'No,' she said, 'not Franz.'

'Why not?'

'It he'd been the traitor he could have revealed everything. He even knew about the metal. He helped at the operation.'

So scrub out Franz. But there was no way of scrubbing out Paula. He could see how sweetly it all fitted in. He did not want to believe it, but he could not be sure it was not true; he could never be sure, not entirely. He had kidded himself that she was in love with him, and maybe she had been playing him along all the time, right from the moment in that room in Torun when she had risen from her chair in that swift, sinuous movement to kiss his mouth. Maybe there had been none of the old magic for her but only a job of work. And all that stuff about Katyn. Maybe she had never had any uncles killed there; maybe it had been nothing but a line she was dishing out. But there was no proof, and he would never know;

239

never for certain.

He noticed that Linda was gazing at him rather thoughtfully. 'Tell me, Steve,' she said, 'was there something going between you and that nice blonde Polish girl?'

Brady shook his head. 'No, nothing. It was just a business deal.' He knew she did not believe him, but what of it?

He heard the kettle boiling, and he went back into the kitchenette and made the tea. He brought it to the table, and she looked up at him and said: 'Don't let it bug you, Steve. Doesn't it make you proud to think you've been walking round with a piece of armour plating inside you like the latest Russian tank?'

'Not noticeably,' Brady said.

He poured the tea, and she took a cup and sipped it. 'Do you remember, Steve, what you were talking about that day I took you to pay off a man named Milligan?'

'Not precisely. Perhaps you'd better jog my memory.'

'You were saying how nice it would be to keep the money and take a holiday for two on the Costa Brava.'

'Yes?'

'You've got four thousand, five hundred and fifty pounds now and you don't owe Milligan a penny.'

'Yes?' Brady said again.

'And I've got some leave coming up.'

Brady drank some tea. 'Am I right in

thinking you've just made me a proposition?'

'If you like to call it that.'

He looked at the money lying on the table. 'There's certainly enough there for a bumper holiday for two.'

'So where shall it be, Steve darling? The French Riviera? Greece? Morocco? The Bahamas?'

'Let's settle for Brighton,' Brady said. 'Frankly, I've had just about as much foreign travel as I can take for the present.'

R

R NE
   NC

6/09